The Little Unicorn

A Journey Within

A Promise of Kindness

No Harm Policy & Disclaimer

Department of Story Preservation
Division of Magical Ethics / Realm of No-Place

No Unicorns were harmed, inconvenienced, or even slightly ruffled in the making of this book. All magical and non-magical creatures involved generously offered their energy and wisdom of their own free will, and have since returned to their respective realms in impeccable spirits. This book contains metaphors, symbolism, terrible cliches, repetitions, predictable twists, repetitions and some misguided humour that probably should've been left out. Interpret gently and at your own risk.

Side effects may include quiet wonder, gentle discomfort, occasional eye rolls, and – most notably – the subtle return of memories you thought long lost. Any resemblance to real Unicorns, living or imaginary, is purely coincidental (but if you do happen to know a real Unicorn, kindly let them know they are dearly missed).

Signed with imaginary ink and maybe a little stardust.

The Collector of Stories on behalf of

Department of Story Preservation / No-Place Division

Words Left Unwritten

Copyright & Publishing

The Little Unicorn
A Journey Within
by **Marcel Gerstel**

COPYRIGHT © 2025 MINDLOOP
WWW.MINDLOOP.COM.AU

WWW.TLUBOOK.COM

ISBN 978-1-7640239-1-7
ABN 94 256 399 396
TLU_IS_012_rev03q

The story you hold is stitched with stars, secret hoof-prints, and a little bit of wonder. Please don't copy it, bottle it, or send it flying across the wind – magic or not – without asking first.

But let's be real – nobody's going to hunt you down if you do. So let me ask nicely: pretty please, don't copy it. These occasional sparkle-pennies are mostly emotional support at this point.

That said, if you're photocopying a page or two to share with your grandma, you have my full blessing. Just don't upload it online – Unicorns are forgiving creatures that believe in second chances, but even they get twitchy when their tails end up in some random download folder called 'misc-stuff.

Marcel
(The Collector of Stories)

Three Decades and a Thousand Echoes

Reflections on 30 Years of The Little Unicorn

It's hard to believe *The Little Unicorn* was born thirty years ago. Back then, I sat cross-legged on the floor of an old shed, scribbling chapter after chapter over the course of several quiet months – completely immersed in a world I didn't yet know would stay with me for decades.

The internet was still in its infancy. Life felt brimming with possibility. I had no map for where this story might lead – only the quiet certainty that it needed to be told. With nothing but pen, paper, and a heart full of stubborn wonder, I wrote in solitude. No smartphones. No feedback loops. Just the hum of imagination, and the occasional spider for company.

Looking back, I realise now that *The Little Unicorn* was never just a story. It was a reflection of my own journey – an exploration of hope, courage, and finding light in the shadows. Stories evolve over time, and so do the people who hold them. What once was scribbled as a beginning now feels like a conversation still unfolding.

This re-imagined edition is a tribute to that moment in time. To the late nights. The self-doubt. The silent trust that even the simplest stories – told quietly and from the heart – can leave a lasting trace. I'm honoured to share this tale with a new generation of readers, as well as those who remember it from its earliest days.

Thank you for being part of the journey – whether you're discovering *The Little Unicorn* for the first time, or returning with soft memories and grown-up eyes.

It was never just a book – it's a piece of my heart. And I hope it becomes a piece of yours, too.

For the Dreamers and the Lost

Dedication

To you – the wanderers, the questioners, the ones who dare to embrace the unknown. To those who seek light in the shadows, courage in uncertainty, and magic in the ordinary. To those who fall, rise, and fall again – and still choose to believe in something beautiful. May this tale remind you of the extraordinary journey within.

To everyone who, knowingly or unknowingly, helped me along the way – thank you. This story exists not just because of you, but for you. It is as much yours as it is mine, and I hope this journey stays with you long after the final page is turned.

And as you embark on your journey, remember...

It's not just the tale. It's the spaces between. That's where quiet things come to life. Some steps are keys. The path reveals itself when you are ready. And not everything is as it seems.

Contents

Does a Unicorn have a horn on its head?

"Yes."

Does such a creature exist?

"No."

For

Twinky

&

Laura Jane

The Little Unicorn

A Journey Within

Not all tales start with

"Once upon a time."

Once upon a time

Nowhere & Everywhere

Arrival at No-Place

▌▌ Suddenly, the world exhaled into darkness. The sun vanished without a whisper of warning, and the vibrant forest below the towering mountain dissolved into shadow. Flowers wilted into faint memories of their bloom, and the once-proud trees crumbled, fading into the vast, silent emptiness. It was as if the world had breathed everything into NOTHING.

The Little Unicorn froze, its shimmering mane rippling with an unearthly light in the eerie stillness. The silence here was louder than[099] usual. Its pearly hooves, so sure moments before, now seemed to hover uncertainly above... something – or perhaps, nothing.

"Where am I?" it asked, the words fragile and uncertain, lingering in the heavy air.

"You are at No-Place," a voice answered, barely more than a thought, its tone as soft as the brush of mist on its skin[023]. The sound seemed to come from everywhere and nowhere at once.

"No-Place?" The Unicorn's head lifted sharply, its coat catching faint, scattered beams in the misty void. "That's impossible! I must be somewhere. There's no such thing as No-Place. Just a moment ago, I was in the forest, surrounded by flowers, with sunlight on my back." It turned, bewildered, its gaze cutting through the empty haze. "Now... I'm here. What happened?"

The voice answered again, its presence not in the air but just behind the Unicorn's thoughts.

"You are here because no one believes in you anymore. Without belief[151], there is no purpose. Without purpose, there is no place. And without place, there is No-Place – the place that is Nowhere."

The words struck like a crashing wave, their weight pulling the Unicorn's head low. Its golden horn, dim but steady, cast a faint light into the shadows. Tears gathered in its deep, expressive eyes, trailing down its cheeks only to vanish before meeting whatever lay below.

"I thought I still had time," the Unicorn whispered, its voice trembling and broken. "I thought someone, somewhere, might still believe in me."

"Do not cry, little one," the voice said softly, its tone gentle and filled with kindness. "No-Place is not what you[129] think. It is the realm of Symbols and Emotions – of all things forgotten but not truly lost. Others dwell here, just like you."

"Others?" The Unicorn blinked away its tears, the faintest glimmer of hope stirring in its heart. "You mean... I'm not alone?"

"Not alone," the voice assured gently. "Come with me, and you will see."

For a moment, it hesitated, its gaze sweeping the endless mist, searching for something – anything – that might anchor it. There was no ground beneath its hooves, no sky above its head – only a thick, pulsing whiteness that seemed to breathe with its own slow rhythm. Each cautious step forward felt like stepping on a cloud, soft yet resistant, as though the mist itself intentionally hindered its progress. But there was nowhere else to go.

Step by step, it pressed on, its horn casting a faint glow that cut through the shifting void. It stalled for an instant, its gaze searching the endless mist, each step burdened with questions too complex to untangle just yet. The silence hung heavy, still and waiting, as if the mist itself were holding its breath. The Unicorn hesitated, its hooves pressing against the nothingness beneath it.

No-Place was silent – too silent. Even the mist, thick and breathing like slow-moving tides, made[181] no sound as it shifted.

It took a step forward, its golden horn sending ripples of light through the lingering darkness.

Somewhere in the distance, something stirred.

Not a sound.

Not a movement.

Just... a shift. Like the way a room feels different when someone has just left it.

A quiet chill brushed[219] against the Unicorn's mane – not cold, not warm, just... present. It turned its head slightly – not enough to look, just enough to listen.

Nothing – the mist remained still, unbothered by the weight of anything unseen. Still, the feeling lingered.

A presence that wasn't there. Or perhaps had just[064] been.*

The Unicorn exhaled slowly and walked on, its heart uncertain why it was beating so fast.

The soft light of its horn was the only comfort – a fragile beacon in a world where[001] nothing else seemed real. It flickered faintly, like a thread of hope refusing to break.

"I hope the others aren't as lost as I feel right now," the young traveller whispered, its voice shaking but steady with determination. The words lingered in the mist for a moment before dissolving, leaving only the faint hum of the endless Nowhere.

*You've only just begun, haven't you?

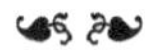

A Love Left Behind

The Little Girl Love

R They had walked for what felt like forever or maybe just a few moments when, OUT of the endless whiteness of No-Place, a figure appeared – a[035] little girl, sitting quietly on nothing. Her golden hair shimmered faintly, though no sunlight was THERE to catch it. Her hands rested limply in her lap, and silvery tears traced lines down her pale cheeks before vanishing into the mist below.

After three more steps, the Little Unicorn stopped abruptly, its head turning sharply toward the faint whisper of the guiding voice. "Wait! She's crying – we have to help her!"

But the voice was silent, swallowed by the stillness. Alone but undeterred, it stepped closer to the girl, its hooves leaving no imprint on the cloud-like ground.

The girl looked up at the sound of the white creature's voice. Her tear-filled eyes, blue like the endless summer sky, startled the Unicorn with their depth. "My name IS Love," she said softly, her voice as delicate as a lullaby. Silvery tears traced her cheeks. "And I[133] am dying."

As its shimmering mane dulled in the still air, the Little Unicorn's heart felt as though it had stopped for a moment. "That's_terrible! There must be something I can do – please, let me help you!"

Love offered a faint, bittersweet smile – the kind that carried a thousand unspoken stories. "No, my friend" she whispered. "There's nothing you can do. I've been fading for a long time. I was shaped into something I was never meant to be, so I ran, hoping to find myself again. But now[163]... no one truly sees me anymore. And so, I am here."

With a slight tilt of its head, the lone Unicorn's large, expressive eyes filled with quiet understanding. A soft glow from its golden horn wrapped around them both. "But it seems so strange... doesn't everyone need love?"

A quiet breath escaped as she gently brushed a strand of golden hair from her face – though even that small movement seemed to drain what little energy Love still retained. "Everyone longs for love, but only when it is simple, effortless. When I no longer fit into their expectations, I became an inconvenience – reshaped, redefined, perceived as selfish or too complicated. If I had stayed, I would have been twisted into an unrecognisable version of myself. And what is Love, if not[196] true to herself?"

Lowering its horn, the creature knelt beside her, its gaze filled with compassion and wonder. "It doesn't make sense... how could they let you fade when they need you so much?"

Love sighed, the sound so soft it barely stirred the mist. "You must understand, needing something isn't the same as cherishing it," she said quietly. "I was needed, but never nurtured. Held too tightly, reshaped and controlled – until I was so drained that nothing of me remained to give. Without care, even the strongest love can fade."

The Unicorn's heart ached. "I still don't understand," it admitted. "I'm here because no one believes in me anymore. But so many still believe in you. How can you be dying?"

After a brief moment of endless silence, Love tilted her head, looking up. "Belief isn't enough," she said softly. "Love needs more than that. It needs kindness to nurture it, patience to let it grow, and truth to keep it genuine. Without these, love withers – losing its strength and, eventually, its purpose."

She sighed, her voice growing fainter. "But too often, love is mistaken for attachment or offered with expectation, as if[223] it should thrive anywhere. That's why I am fading."

Reaching out, she touched the Unicorn's mane, her frail fingers barely brushing the shimmering strands. "Listen carefully. You need to understand this for your journey. Like many others, I'm not perfect, but I am whole. I make mistakes – many mistakes – but that, too, is part of who I am. For true love isn't flawless; it's honest. It cannot reshape itself to meet expectations and remain true."

The gentle being nodded slowly, though its thoughts were still tangled. "Is there nothing I can do to help you?" it asked again, its voice trembling.

Love's faint smile returned, warmer this time, like the soft glow of a fading star. "There is. Keep going. Find the others, and remind them who they are. If you[100] do that, maybe I'll find my strength again. But don't linger here for me. What will be, will be."

The Unicorn hesitated, unwilling to leave but sensing the finality in her tone. "Goodbye, Love," it said softly.

When it finally turned back, it realised – too late – that it had forgotten to say one last thing. But Love was gone, leaving only emptiness where she had been, as though she had never been there at all.

Staring back at the spot, the Unicorn's thoughts remained tangled in emotions too complex to name[054]. "Love is strange," it said softly. "We never see where it begins, but we always know when it ends."

As it continued on, a faint warmth brushed against its mane – like the lingering touch of sunlight. Though Love was gone, a part of her presence remained, fragile yet enduring – a quiet reminder that even in fading, she had left something behind. Something that endured.

In the world it had left behind, Love had become elusive – like a reflection in a raindrop, gone before it could be traced. But here, in No-Place, she was different: fragile, yet undeniably REAL. The Unicorn vowed to carry her memory forward, for as long as it could.

❧ ☙

The Truth No One Wants

A Man Named Honesty

E The Little Unicorn wandered through the endless whiteness of No-Place, the silence pressing close from all sides. Love's fragile words lingered in its thoughts, filling its heart with a strange mix of sorrow and longing.

"She might make it," the voice said suddenly, breaking the heavy stillness.

"What did YOU say?" the Unicorn asked, turning sharply.

"Love," the voice repeated, faint but steady. "She might make it. Love is strong and full of surprises. Sometimes, when you think you've lost her, when you think she's gone, she reappears right where you least expect her. Love always finds a way."

Even though these words sparked a flicker of hope, the hooved wanderer chose silence. Lowering its head, it pressed forward, the soft glow of its horn carving a path through the mist.

After what felt like hours – or maybe just a few minutes; time was slippery here* – a figure emerged in the distance. A young man sat slouched on a bright yellow rock that shimmered like sunlight trapped in stone. His head rested heavily in his hands, as though weighed down by invisible burdens.

"Welcome to No-Place," the man said, his voice calm but touched with exhaustion. He looked up, revealing piercing green eyes framed by a face both kind and worn. "What brings you to my humble home?" he asked.

"I'm not entirely sure," the Unicorn admitted. "I think I'm here because no one believes in me anymore. I've been told[095] to meet the Emotions who live here – maybe they have the answers I need. Who ARE you?"

The man gave a faint, uneven smile. "My name is Honesty, but you can call me Lie – everyone else does. It's a bit shorter and much easier for them, I suppose."

Puzzled, the young Unicorn asked, "Lie? Why would anyone call you that?"

Honesty shrugged, running a hand through his unkempt hair. "I think I make things uncomfortable. I'm called upon when it's convenient, but the moment I arrive, I'm pushed away. 'Too inconvenient,' they say. 'Too painful.' 'Too difficult.' And so, over time, I've become nothing more than a shadow of myself. So here I sit, waiting for someone who truly wants me. But no one ever does."

"That's not true!" the Unicorn protested, stepping closer. "I like you, Honesty. And I'm sure I'm not THE only one. I think you're wonderful – honestly, Honesty."

Honesty's smile grew a touch warmer, though his eyes stayed heavy. "Thank you, little one. But sadly, not everyone feels the same. Most of them prefer comfort over truth. It's easier for them that way."

The Unicorn hesitated, its thoughts twisting and tangling like loose threads in the breeze. "Have you seen Love?" it asked at last. "I met her earlier, but she didn't seem well."

Honesty's expression darkened, his gaze drifting to the mist below. "Yes, I saw her. She passed through here some time ago. Love and I share much in common – we're both misunderstood, both difficult to hold on to. But despite how fragile she seems, Love is strong. Stronger than I am, in many ways. She may yet surprise us all."

The thought of Love fading made the Unicorn's heart tighten. It stood in quiet contemplation, watching Honesty. The soft glow of his yellow rock cut through the mist, its warmth strangely out of place in the endless grey.

As if from nowhere, the Unicorn suddenly said, "You're not what I expected."

Honesty glanced over in surprise, raising an eyebrow. "What exactly were you expecting?"

"I'm not sure. Maybe someone... simpler? You carry too much – too much truth, too many answers, too many things to face all at once."

Honesty let out a quiet laugh, though there was little humour in it. "Truth is always simple, little one – it just rarely looks that way."

Before[065] the Unicorn could respond, the voice returned.

"We must go now."

"Wait!" the pearl-hooved traveller called out, turning back to Honesty. "I'm not finished talking to him!"

Honesty raised a hand in farewell, a nostalgic_smile on his lips. "Goodbye," he said. "If you ever need me, just remember – I'll always be here for those who look for me."

Reluctantly, the Unicorn turned to follow the voice. Glancing back one last time, it saw only the yellow rock, glowing faintly against the infinite white. Honesty was gone.

"Don't worry about him," the voice said gently. "He comes and goes, though he should stay. Honesty isn't always easy – sometimes, he's hard to face – but deep down, all he truly wants is to do what's right."

A pause.

Then – a whisper where there should have been silence.

"Wait. You can hear me, can't you?"

A flicker, a hesitation.

"No, that's ridiculous... you shouldn't be able to. And yet... here you are."

A long breath, a shift in weight. Then, softer – "It's me – Honesty. I don't know how else to say this, but... I was made for this. Written into it. I exist only because someone decided I should."

"That yellow rock?" A small, almost[033] bitter laugh. "It's not real. Nothing here is."

A pause, like something unseen pressing at the edges of the world.

"They don't know that yet. The others. I can't tell them. They believe it's all real, and ...honestly – no pun intended..." A faint smile in the voice, but something behind it unsettled. "I don't have the heart to take that away from them."

"So I'll wait. Let them find out on their own, if they ever do. But you? You already see it, don't you?"

Another silence – this one heavier.

"I wonder... what will you do with this truth?"

A breath. A flicker of something unseen.

Then – "Now, if you don't mind, I'll go back and return to my 'yellow rock'... and let them return you to the story."

Walking in silence, the Unicorn's thoughts circled the yellow rock and the man who sat upon it. "Doing the right thing is harder than it seems," it said quietly, more to itself than to the voice. "The line between right and wrong is rarely as clear as we'd like it to be."

Its hooves moved lightly, the faint glow of its horn flickering against the endless white. Though Honesty was gone, his presence lingered – a quiet reminder of the simple yet complicated beauty of truth.

*You've been reading for a while now.
Have you noticed how time is moving different here?

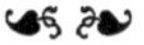

Marching Into the Mist

War

As the Little Unicorn ventured deeper into No-Place, a shadowy figure emerged at the edge of the mist. The silhouette stood bold and imposing, like a dark boundary cutting through the misty softness. It did[034] not move, yet its presence hung heavy in the air, uninviting and oppressive.

A ripple of uncertainty rose within as the young Unicorn hesitantly asked, "Who is that?"

"Oh, him?" the voice replied, softer[098] now, as if not wanting to be overheard. "He doesn't belong here. There is a place for him – far from peace, in the heart of conflict – but he refuses to stay there. Go on, ask him yourself."

Gathering all its courage, the Unicorn hesitated before stepping closer. Its hooves felt as though they were sinking into the mist, yet curiosity pulled it forward. As the distance closed, the figure took shape – an old General, his faded uniform weighed down by medals of every size and colour. Once brilliant, they now appeared tarnished, like memories left too long in the sun. Two oversized golden stars sat on the breast of his jacket, absurdly large, as if desperate to command admiration.

"A-T-T-E-N-T-I-O-N!" he barked suddenly, his voice cracking like a whip through the stillness.

The Unicorn briefly jumped, its horn instantly glowing brighter in alarm, before quickly collecting itself. "Careful!" it warned, pointing to the edge where[006] the man's boot hovered dangerously close to nothingness. "Watch your step – you might slip and fall!"

The General let out a dry, humourless chuckle, adjusting his cap with a hand that trembled – just enough to notice. "Slip? Fall? Not me, Soldier. I live on the edge. It's where I[004] thrive." He straightened slightly, his voice carrying a hint of pride. "Name's War, by the way. And don't you[224] worry about me – I've got my footing just fine."

Turning its head slightly, its shimmering mane caught the faint light from its horn. "I'm not a soldier," the young Unicorn said softly. "The ground beneath you looks fragile, and the edges may not hold your weight, Mr. War. Aren't you[066] afraid of falling?"

War's laugh was sharp and joyless, rattling like hollow bones. "Afraid? Why would I be afraid? I've seen it all! And then I was cast aside, left to fade like a forgotten relic. But it never lasts. I am always needed again. I always am."

The Unicorn stepped closer, cautious. "Why would anyone need you when all you bring is suffering?"

War straightened, his medals clinking faintly as he puffed out his chest. "Because they believe they do. When fear takes hold, when greed whispers in their ear, when they crave more than they have, they turn to me. They call[130] with trembling hands, convincing themselves they are in control. But they never are."

Its golden horn dimming, its face drawn into a frown, the young, courageous traveller turned to War. "But doesn't that just hurt them in the end?"

War leaned down, his intense stare locking onto the Unicorn's wide eyes. His voice dropped to a venomous hiss. "Hurt them? Perhaps. But I also distract them – from their fears, their failures, themselves. I give them a sense of control, even if it's an illusion. I give them power, purpose, and pride. And tell me, isn't a little pain, a little suffering, a small price to pay?"

He straightened once more, his cold gaze steady. "So when they call for me, I answer. I never disappoint. And I never truly disappear."

The Unicorn shivered, stepping back as its mane trembled. "You... you shouldn't exist at all."

War's thunderous laughter erupted again, sharp and echoing, wrapping around the mist like a coiled snake. "Shouldn't exist? Ha! As long as one person believes in me, I'll exist. And trust me, little one, someone..."

He stopped.

His piercing eyes suddenly shifted – not toward the Unicorn, but just past it, over its left shoulder. And his gaze lingered – just an instant too long.

For a moment, his expression shifted. It wasn't anger, arrogance, or even amusement. It was something else – a flicker of something questioning, unreadable.

"Hmph," he muttered, his voice lower now, almost to himself. "For a moment, I thought..."

A sharp shake of his head, a quick, forced breath through his nose.

And just like that, War was War again.

"...someone always does."

The Unicorn blinked. It wasn't sure what had just happened. Had something... moved behind it? Though the mist lay still, something unseen pressed against the air – like a breath held too long, waiting to be released.

War's sharp gaze returned to the Unicorn, his presence once more unshaken, as though nothing had happened at all. And for the briefest moment, his sharp eyes softened – not with kindness, but with something heavier. But the change was fleeting. He turned toward the void beyond the edge of No-Place.

"Excuse me," he said, his voice low and icy. "Someone is calling. It seems I'm needed once again."

Without[167] another word, War stepped off the edge. He dropped like a rusted cannonball, vanishing swiftly into the mist below. His mocking laughter clung to the air, long after he was gone.

The Unicorn's mane grew just a little paler, rippling as if trying to shake off a lingering chill. With a shiver, it whispered, "What a horrible character," its voice still trembling.

The guiding voice returned, quiet and reflective. "Horrible, yes. But he exists because he was created. As long as he is trusted, he will[193] never truly fade away."

As the young traveller walked on, trotting lightly over the misty ground, its heart grew heavier. War's shadow loomed large in its thoughts – a grim reminder that darkness lingered not just in No-Place, but in the world beyond as well.

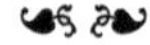

Trampled Beauty

The Daisy Dignity

L The Little Unicorn stared at the spot where War had stood moments before disappearing into the mist. As[197] it gazed closer, something small and delicate caught its eye – a tiny white daisy, crushed and bent under the weight of War's boots.

Lowering its head, the Unicorn studied the fragile flower with quiet curiosity. Its petals were torn and bruised, its slender stem leaning to one side, barely able to hold itself upright.

"War stood on me," the daisy said softly, its voice trembling like the faintest whisper in a quiet breeze. "But I'm used to it[135]. It happens all the time."

The Unicorn blinked, startled. "That's awful..." it said gently.

"My name is Dignity," the flower began with a sigh and a hint of frustration in its voice. "And I've been stepped on for as long as I[170] can remember. More soles have pressed against me than souls have truly seen me."

The daisy's words lingered heavy. "But you're so beautiful, why would anyone step on you?"

"I was never truly seen for what I am," she said, her voice laced with quiet resignation. "Some have tried to claim me as something they could possess, while others have trampled over me without a second[076] thought. But you must understand this – Dignity cannot be stolen. It can only be given away. And once it's gone, life becomes truly miserable."

After letting the daisy's words settle, it spoke with quiet resolve. "I won't give you away, Dignity. You're far too important."

Dignity's petals trembled faintly, as if unsure whether to trust such a promise. "Then take care," she whispered. "I'm more fragile inside than I seem on the outside."

As it looked around, the Unicorn spotted a small stick lying on the misty ground – or whatever passed for ground in No-Place. Lowering its[009] head, it carefully picked up the stick with its mouth and, with precise movements, gently tied it to the daisy's bent stem, steadying it upright.

"There you go!" it said, stepping back to admire its work. "This will help you stand tall until you find your roots again."

The daisy's petals seemed to brighten, lifting slightly as though reaching for a sun that wasn't there. "Thank you, my friend," she said softly. "You've given me hope. And now, I wish you farewell. Always remember – no matter what happens, hold onto me. Never give me away."

"Farewell, Dignity," the Unicorn replied, stepping back. A quiet warmth began to spread through its chest. For the first time since arriving in[068] No-Place, it felt a small sense of peace. Helping the daisy had eased some of the weight in its heart, if only for a moment.

As it walked away, it noticed something remarkable. The crushing sorrow it had carried since entering No-Place felt lighter, replaced by a steady, comforting glow. A quiet realisation bloomed within – it had begun to heal, not just by moving forward, but by helping others along the way.

"Help is like a river," the Little Unicorn said quietly. "The more it flows outward, the more it is replenished by unseen springs."

The path ahead still stretched endlessly, wrapped in the misty silence of No-Place. Yet, the Unicorn felt a flicker[036] of hope – not for what lay ahead, but for the difference small acts of kindness could make.

FIFTY-ONE

Flickers in the Dark

A Sparkle of Hope

I "You've helped her a lot, my young friend," the voice said, softer now, like a gentle breeze brushing against the Unicorn's mane. "But there's someone else I want you to meet[194]. Look over there."

The golden-horned traveller followed the voice's direction, curiosity stirring once more. Its gaze swept toward where the voice had pointed, but only darkness met its eyes. Squinting into the void, it finally noticed a tiny golden sparkle, hovering delicately just above the surface – if such a thing could even exist in[037] No-Place.

"Who... who are you?" the Unicorn asked hesitantly, its voice filled with wonder.

A faint, distant reply came, trembling as though carried from a faraway dream. "I am Hope... though now, I am but the smallest sparkle I have ever been."

The Unicorn stepped closer, its golden horn casting a faint glow as if competing with the light of the sparkle. "But you're so small. I'm afraid even the softest breath might carry you away."

"They told me I was nothing. And I believed them. But nothing is impossible – so don't underestimate me," Hope replied, its voice growing steadier. "Even the smallest spark can light the way. But I was not always like this. Once, I burned with flames so bright they could turn the deepest night into day[191] and banish even the most stubborn shadows. Now... I am but a glimmer."

"How did this happen?" the Unicorn asked, its heart pounding with quiet curiosity.

Hope paused, as if carefully shaping the right words. "It began when I gave pieces of myself to those in need. I trusted that my light would be shared once the healing had taken place. But instead, it was held too tightly – clutched, hoarded, always taken, never released. And that's how I faded."

"Is there anything we[159] can do to keep you shining?" the Unicorn asked, its voice trembling.

Hope hesitated. "I don't know my young friend. There were times when I thought I could never fade. But the[069] world has changed, and now... I'm no longer certain."

Suddenly, a brilliant streak of light shot through the void, like the brightest shooting star piercing the darkness. The Little Unicorn lowered its head, shielding its eyes. When it looked up again, Hope had grown into a steady, golden glow, casting soft rays of warmth into the mist.

"What just happened?" it asked, eyes wide with amazement.

"Someone gave me back a piece of myself," Hope said warmly, her voice steadier, stronger. "Someone, somewhere, found contentment in what they had. And now, a part of my strength has returned."

"Will you keep it this time?" the Unicorn asked.

Hope's glow shimmered with quiet laughter. "Of course not. It's not my nature to keep it. I pass my light to those who need it more than I do."

As Hope began to release its light, the Little Unicorn noticed something unusual beyond the glow. "Wait[005]! What is that behind you?"

The sparkle shifted slightly, revealing a towering shape in the distance – a mass of metal and light, glinting faintly in the golden rays. "That is the Mountain of Keys," Hope explained. "A place of great importance, guarded by Freedom – the one you must meet. Come, I will light the way."

Hesitating, the Unicorn stared up at the distant mountain. Though it[102] towered far ahead, Hope's glow stretched toward it, forming a shimmering path through the mist. Step by step, the Unicorn followed, drawn forward by the quiet pull of something unseen.

At first, the ground was smooth beneath its hooves, but as they neared the base of the mountain, the terrain shifted – cool metal replacing the misty ground of No-Place. The Unicorn took a deep breath and stepped onto the first of many keys, their surfaces shifting slightly under its weight.

Hope's warm glow flickered ahead, steady and reassuring. "Keep going," came the gentle encouragement. "You are meant to climb this."

Climbing hoof by hoof, the Unicorn pressed forward, feeling a quiet reassurance as they ascended together. Watching the tiny spark grow into a beacon filled its heart with awe. The light wove a path upward, as if it knew exactly where to go. Each step felt lighter, steadier.

"Thank you," the Unicorn whispered as they neared the summit. But when it turned to speak again, Hope was gone – vanishing into a streak of light that disappeared into the void.

Though it felt a touch[128] of sadness, it also felt something new and powerful. It glanced back at the path they had travelled, where Hope's lingering glow still faintly marked the way.

"Even the smallest spark can make a difference," the Unicorn said, its voice filled with quiet determination. Turning its gaze toward the mountain's peak, it added softly, "I won't forget that."

Burdens of Maybe

The Shadow of Doubt and Uncertainty

T As the Little Unicorn walked away from Hope's last lingering glow, a chill crept into the air. The mist of No-Place thickened, wrapping around the path as if determined to obscure the way forward. Twisted shapes emerged and[236] faded in the haze. The Unicorn's hooves grew heavier with each step, as though the very ground resisted its journey.

"You think[101] you've made progress?" a soft, mocking voice whispered eerily, slipping through the mist like an icy breath. "How naive."

"Who's there?" the Unicorn demanded, firm despite the tremor in its voice.

From the shadows, a_figure emerged – formless and ever-shifting, its edges rippling like ink spilled into water. It twisted and shifted, breaking apart and reforming, as if caught between identities, indecisive and restless.

"I[172] am The Shadow of Doubt and Uncertainty," it said, its tone smooth and venomous, dripping with contempt. "I've been with you all along, watching as you stumble blindly through this journey."

As the Unicorn stepped back, its hooves sank slightly into the ground. "I'm not stumbling," it said, though a flicker of uncertainty laced its words. "I'm helping the Emotions. I've made progress."

The Shadow let out a brittle, fractured laugh, the sound like dry leaves crushed under a heavy boot. "Helping? Do you truly believe that? Or are you just wandering aimlessly, clutching at the edges of a[139] purpose you'll never find?"

Its chest tightened as the Shadow's words crept into its mind like long, bony fingers of mist. For a moment, it felt paralysed, the weight of darkness pressing in. The mist thickened around it, swirling in time with the Shadow's voice, as if echoing its contempt.

"Did you think Hope could save you?" the Shadow sneered, slithering closer. "That tiny spark is already fading. And when it's gone, you'll be left with nothing but me."

The Unicorn briefly closed its eyes, Hope's warm light flickering faintly in its memory. "Even a single spark can light the way". The words glowed softly in its mind, pushing back against the Shadow's creeping strands.

With a much steadier voice, the Unicorn said firmly, "I don't need you," each word slicing through the suffocating mist. "You're not real[002]. You're just my fears trying to hold me back."

The Shadow rippled, its darkness tightening into a jagged, pulsing mass, feeding on the young creatures lingering doubt. "I am as real as the doubt in your heart," it hissed. "I am your hesitation, your questions – the pause before every step you take, before every word you speak. And I will always be here, waiting."

Standing taller, the young traveller's horn flickered brightly. Each pulse of light pushed back the darkness, illuminating the shifting mist. "You can wait all you want," it said firmly, quiet strength rising in its voice. "But you'll never stop[067] me."

The Shadow of Doubt and Uncertainty recoiled, its edges quivering as though weakened by the[038] Unicorn's resolve. "We'll see," it whispered, its voice growing faint as it dissolved into the mist. "We'll see..."

The mist thinned slightly, its suffocating weight easing just enough to reveal the path ahead. The air itself seemed to pause, as if drawing a slow, relieved breath[010]. Though its hooves still trembled faintly, a quiet determination began to take root. "Doubt will always be there," the Unicorn murmured to itself, its golden horn flickering steadily. "But it doesn't have to lead the way."

With that, it stepped forward, its hooves light against the metal covered ground. Though the Shadow's whisper still lingered in the air, the Unicorn clung to Hope's words – a[198] spark that could not be swallowed by the dark.

SIXTY-THREE

Lost Keys, Forgotten Doors

Freedom and the Mountain of Keys

Y "So this is the Mountain of Keys," the Unicorn remarked, its gaze climbing the towering peak. The mountain stretched higher than it had imagined, its surface glittering with hues of gold, silver, and rust. Keys of every shape and size spilled downward in a shimmering cascade – like a frozen waterfall of forgotten[162] possibilities.

Taking another cautious step forward, the Unicorn's hoof landed with a delicate *'clink'*. Looking down, it finally realised – the mountain truly was made entirely of keys. Some were rusted and twisted with age, while others gleamed as if freshly forged. Their sheer abundance was staggering, cascading endlessly upward in a[040] shimmering metallic stream.

The Unicorn ascended carefully, its hooves causing the keys to shift beneath each step. The soft jingling created a melody – haunting and strangely soothing. Now, a mere eight steps from the summit, it[106] felt a faint presence waiting above, silently urging it onward.

"These must be all the keys that were cast away," it wondered. "But why would anyone throw them away?"

"They thought they didn't need them," a calm voice replied from above.

Startled, the Unicorn looked up. Near the summit sat a young man, his delicate white wings wrapped tightly in thick, heavy bandages. His face was calm, but faint lines of struggle and sorrow etched his features.

"You must be Freedom," the Unicorn said as it climbed closer.

The figure nodded. "That I am. And I see you've made it to my mountain. Do watch your step – it's easy to lose your hooving when the ground holds[008] so many secrets."

The Unicorn paused to steady itself, its golden horn casting a faint glow. Its gaze landed on the bandages wrapped around his wings. "What happened to your wings?" it asked, its heart aching at the sight.

"Glancing at his back, Freedom couldn't hide the dry smile tugging at his lips. "Oh, these? A little thank-you gift. I wasn't meant to fly back where I came from, so this was how I was kept... grounded."

The Unicorn frowned. "But why would anyone cast you aside? Doesn't everyone want freedom?"

Freedom's smile widened, a glint of dry humour in his eyes. "Oh, they say they do. They love the idea of me. But when it comes down to it, most prefer their cages – especially if they've decorated them nicely. Throw in a rug, a comfy chair, maybe a picture or two on the walls, and suddenly, they're perfectly content."

"But these keys," the Unicorn said, "they could unlock the cages, couldn't they?"

Freedom nodded, gesturing to the shimmering mountain around them. "They could. But the thing about keys is, they only work if you use them. And, well... using a key means admitting you were locked up in the first place. That's a truth most would rather avoid."

The Unicorn lowered its head, sadness settling over it. "That's terrible. How can anyone live without you? How can life exist without freedom?"

"Some call[134] it security," Freedom said with a shrug. "I call it a very dull way to live. But don't feel too bad for me – at least I've got plenty of keys for company. You wouldn't believe the stories some of these hold."

"Do I have a key?" the Little Unicorn asked, curiosity flickering in its voice.

Freedom's smile softened. "You do. A lovely one, in fact. And as long as you don't lose it, you'll always have a way out of any cage you find yourself in. Just remember – there is also a lock on the inside."

The Unicorn hesitated, its gaze drifting to the horizon. "Will your wings ever heal?"

Freedom's face grew distant. He paused a moment too long – like someone caught between this place and a distant memory. "In time," he said, "but my wounds will[230] heal faster than theirs. Some hearts have locked themselves so tightly, they've forgotten they hold the key. But I've learned to wait. Time has a way of surprising you."

He glanced toward the horizon, where the mist of No-Place began to thin. In the distance, a faint, rhythmic sound echoed – a gentle, rolling hush[070], like a breath too heavy with sorrow to fully exhale. "Just like the Ocean of Tears," he said, his voice quieter now. "Its waters remember what the world tries to forget."

The Unicorn followed his gaze, drawn toward the soft shimmer on the horizon. "The Ocean of Tears?" it asked.

Freedom nodded. "Follow its shores, and you may find someone who understands the cost of holding on too tightly."

Beyond the mountain, the misty expanse was suddenly alive with floating orbs of colour, shimmering like soap bubbles caught in pale light. Had they just appeared – in that brief moment when no one was watching the horizon? Or had they always been there, waiting quietly, unnoticed until the right moment arrived?

"What are those?" the Unicorn asked, its voice hushed with wonder.

"Dreams," Freedom said simply. "Broken and abandoned. Left behind to drift here, waiting for someone to hold them again[195]. But they're delicate. Handle with care, or *'poof'* – they're gone."

Staring at the orbs, the Unicorn felt a quiet heaviness settling in its heart. "Is there any way to save them?"

"Maybe," Freedom said gently. "But for now, just keep moving. Sometimes, the best way to help is by learning to let go. Don't worry – dreams are patient. Well... most of them."

The Unicorn nodded, taking one last look at the mountain and its guardian. "Thank you – truly. For reminding me that no lock is without a key."

Freedom smiled, his gaze steady. "And remember – never lose your key. Without it, doors don't just stay closed; they fade, until you forget they ever existed."

SEVENTY-ONE

The Fog of Uncertainty

Whispers in the Mist

As the Unicorn descended the Mountain of Keys, a chill crept into the air. The mist thickened, curling around the[205] path like grasping hands, dense and suffocating. The colourful orbs in the distance seemed to retreat, their light flickering weakly as though struggling to stay alive.

"You think you've done something meaningful?" a soft, mocking voice sneered, slipping through the mist – cool and sharp as morning frost. "All you did was listen to a broken-winged DREAMER. What could you possibly learn from him? He was_forgotten long ago."

The Unicorn froze, its ears flattening against its head. "I learned that even when[071] the world turns against you, you can keep going," it said, though its voice trembled. "Freedom showed me that strength comes from within."

"Freedom?" The Shadow of Doubt AND Uncertainty emerged, its shifting form twisting with restless energy. It flickered erratically, its jagged edges unravelling and reforming as if pulled in conflicting directions. "He's no Freedom," THE Shadow hissed, its tone drenched with mockery. "He's just a relic – discarded and broken. Do you really think his 'keys' can unlock anything? Or are you too blind to see the[143] futility of it all?"

Doubt pressed against the Little Unicorn's heart like a crushing weight. The mist curled closer, heavy with deceit, whispering faint echoes of the Shadow's words. Its golden horn dimmed, its flickering light struggling against the consuming darkness.

"Do you feel it?" the Shadow hissed, circling the intimidated creature like a predator. "That crack in your certainty? That tiny voice wondering if I might be right? You think you're strong, but your strength is built[148] on nothing more than fragile hope. And hope, little one, breaks so easily."

For a moment, the Unicorn's chest tightened, the weight of the Shadow's words clawing at its courage. But then it remembered Freedom's parting message: "Every cage has a key."

"I believe in that," the Unicorn said, its voice steadying as its golden horn began to glow faintly. "And I believe in myself," it added humbly.

The Shadow rippled, its darkness thickening like a storm cloud. "Believe all you want," it spat, its voice low and venomous. "Beliefs crumble under the weight of reality[007]. I'll be here, waiting in the shadows. I always will."

Standing taller now, the Unicorn's light grew brighter. "Then wait," it said firmly, its voice cutting through the mist. "But I'll keep moving forward – with or without your whispers."

The Shadow's jagged edges flickered as though caught in its own turmoil. It recoiled slightly, shifting between density and emptiness, as if unsure whether to attack or retreat. Finally, it dissolved into[109] the mist, its presence lingering like an icy chill that refused to fully fade.

The Unicorn stood still, gathering its strength. Its chest rose and fell slowly as the weight of the Shadow's presence began to ease. Turning its gaze back to the horizon, it saw the shimmering orbs dancing faintly in the distance, their fragile light like a promise waiting to be fulfilled.

Taking a deep breath[041], the Unicorn whispered, "Even if doubt lingers, I'll keep moving forward."

And it did.

Pieces of Yesterday

Broken Dreams

X Descending the Mountain of Keys, the Unicorn's gaze was drawn to the shimmering orbs of light hovering over the horizon. They floated in[042] the mist, glowing with every imaginable colour – shifting, swirling, and pulsing like tiny, living round rainbows. The closer it came, the more it realised how vast their number was. Thousands – no, millions – of them drifted aimlessly, fragile yet mesmerising.

"Are they really[226] dreams?" its voice hushed with wonder.

"They are," the guiding voice replied softly. "Dreams that were abandoned. Some slipped away when belief faded, others were lost because they were left unnurtured, uncared for."

Approaching the edge of the horizon, where the orbs hovered closest to the ground, the Unicorn watched as one of the glowing bubbles began to rise, drifting higher and higher into the misty sky. Then, with the faintest, most sorrowful *'pop'*, it burst into a fine, shimmering haze – dissolving into nothingness.

"Did you see that?" the Unicorn cried out, its heart sinking. "It just... vanished."

"That is what happens when a DREAM is forgotten," the voice explained. "Dreams cannot survive on their own. They need someone to hold them, nurture them, and believe in them. Without that, they fade away, leaving only a shadow[199] of sorrow_and a misty memory behind."

The Unicorn's gaze shifted to the other orbs, now floating silently in the mist. Each ONE seemed to carry its own light, its own quiet story. "But why would anyone let go of something so beautiful?" it asked, its voice thick with sadness.

"Because dreams are fragile," the voice answered. "Many are lost in the pursuit of something else, set aside for later until they fade away. Some slip away out of fear – fear of failure, fear of not[011] being enough. Others drift into the distance, abandoned for convenience, waiting to be reclaimed but too often forgotten. And once they are gone, they rarely return."

As the young creature listened, another bubble drifted upward. Its glow dimmed, flickering once before vanishing with a faint '*pop*'. The haze it left behind fell like silent tears into the void below.

"I don't want this to happen to mine," the Unicorn said firmly, its golden horn glowing brighter. "I don't want to lose my dreams."

"Then hold on to them," the voice encouraged. "Dreams may be delicate, but when cherished, they are resilient. Keep them close, and they'll light your way when the path grows dark."

As it turned to continue its journey, something caught the Unicorn's eye – a particularly large bubble hovering just above the ground. Its surface shimmered with a luminous glow, and within it, the Unicorn saw a faint reflection of itself – standing beneath a brilliant sun in a lush green forest. The image pulsed with quiet warmth, a whisper of something distant yet deeply familiar.

"This one feels like a part of me." it whispered, stepping closer. "Is this... my dream[210]?" Its voice trembled with awe.

The voice remained silent, leaving the Unicorn to wonder. Slowly, it extended its golden horn and gently touched the bubble's surface. A ripple spread across the orb, and the dream began to rise, its light growing brighter as it ascended into the sky. Its colours deepened, illuminating the mist with a soft glow before disappearing into the distance.

The Unicorn's gaze lingered on the shimmering bubbles, its heart heavy with[145] the thought of dreams fading into the void.

"But if these are dreams that were abandoned... why is one of mine here? I haven't let go of my dreams."

The voice hesitated, its tone softening. "Not all dreams here are abandoned. Some come to No-Place when they're at risk – when doubt begins to creep in, or when their dreamer starts to question their worth. They linger here, fragile and uncertain, waiting to see whether they will be held or forgotten."

The Unicorn's horn flickered faintly as the realisation settled. "So my dream wasn't taken from me... it drifted here when I began to doubt?"

"Even the strongest hearts can falter," the voice said gently. "What matters is what you[072] choose to do now."

With resolve growing stronger, the Unicorn spoke with a steady voice. "I will not[104] let go of my dreams."

Standing still[169], the young wanderer observed in silence until its dream became a distant sparkle in the sky. A quiet hope bloomed in its chest. Though the horizon remained filled with countless fragile orbs, the Unicorn now understood the importance of holding onto dreams – cherishing what truly mattered... and accepting that some dreams are meant to remain unfulfilled.

With one last glance at the shimmering horizon, the Unicorn turned and continued on its way, carrying its dreams securely within its heart.

Waves of Tears

The Gravel Road of Belief near the Ocean of Tears

I Its journey brought the little Unicorn to a peculiar and daunting path – a winding gravel road stretching endlessly in both directions. The air here felt dense and heavy, carrying the weight of countless unspoken questions. The road was littered with crossroads, each splitting into unknown and uncertain directions. Deep puddles[119] and dark pits lined the gravel path, their edges sharp and uninviting, silently waiting for an unwary traveller to slip and stumble.

"What a strange and unusual path to walk," the Little Unicorn wondered, its steps cautious and deliberate.

"This is the Gravel Road of Belief," the guiding voice replied, its tone calm and serious. "It's a difficult road to walk, filled with choices, doubts, and distractions. Many travel it, but few truly understand its nature. You must tread carefully here."

Moving forward, its hooves sent small stones skittering across the uneven surface. The road quickly revealed its deceptive nature – some crossroads appeared inviting but led to dead ends[003], while others shifted unpredictably, offering no clear way forward.

"I don't like this road," the Unicorn admitted, shaking its head. "It's confusing and far too danger-ous. How is anyone meant to walk it safely?"

"Few do," the voice said quietly. "Some become lost, trapped by indecision. Others stumble into the depths, unable to climb back out alone. And some press forward – determined, yet burdened – unsure of where the road will lead."

The Unicorn paused, its gaze drifting to the vibrant green grass growing along the edges of the gravel. Cautiously, it stepped off the path onto the soft, welcoming blades. Immediately, a sense of relief washed over it.

"This is so much better," the young creature exclaimed, its tension melting away as it glanced back at the harsh gravel. "Why doesn't everyone walk here instead?"

"The road itself is a choice," the voice explained. "Some believe they must stay on it, thinking it's the only way forward, while others are so focused on their struggles that they never notice the grass at all."

Feeling lighter, the Unicorn followed the grassy edge alongside the road, its hooves almost skipping over the soft earth. The oppressive weight of the gravel path began to ease. As it moved forward, the road gradually dissolved into an[201] endless, shimmering expanse – the Ocean of Tears.

The water stretched to the horizon, its surface rippling gently as waves rolled toward the shore. The air held a deep, quiet stillness, as if the[043] world itself were holding its breath.

"It's even more vast than I imagined," the Unicorn thought, a sense of awe settling in its mind.

Every tear ever shed finds its way here, joining countless others on an endless journey toward peace. But peace is not a destination – it is a longing, ebbing and flowing, never truly at rest.

The young traveller stepped closer to the shore, its golden hooves pressing into[233] the soft earth. The waves brushed gently against the edges of the lush grass, their rhythm steady and soothing. For a MOMENT, the Unicorn felt a strange mixture of sorrow and comfort, as though the ocean carried the weight of all the sadness it had[107] ever known, yet somehow lessened its burden.

It turned to the voice, speaking softly. "Will this ocean always be here?"

"Of course, my young companion," the voice replied. "As long as tears exist in the world, the ocean[154] will remain. It is vast, inevitable, and unending.

It watched as its golden horn reflected faintly on the water's surface. Within the ripples, it thought it saw something – faces, fleeting memories, and fragments of forgotten stories. The images danced and faded, like whispers of what was lost.

Then, without warning, the water shuddered. A single ripple spiralled outward in perfect, deliberate circles – too smooth, too precise, as if something unseen had touched it.

Like a fingertip pressing gently against the surface. Testing it. Ensuring it was real.

The Unicorn felt its breath pause. It stepped back, ears twitching, waiting for an explanation that never came.

Then – another ripple. Slow. Measured. The surface trembled as if something beneath had stirred, pressing just close enough to be felt but not yet seen.

A hush fell over the Ocean of Tears, the water once again still. But the silence felt different now. Too deep. Too aware.

The Unicorn's heart pounded. It was not alone.

It stood frozen for a moment, ears straining for a sound, eyes searching the distance for movement – anything. But the water remained still, as if whatever had stirred had already slipped away.

Its breath steadied, though unease lingered at the edges of its thoughts. Slowly, it turned its gaze back to the vast ocean, watching the endless ripples – familiar, yet unchanged – drift into the unknown.

"What happens to the tears once they reach this place?" the Unicorn asked, its voice once again soft and thoughtful.

"They merge with the waves and continue their search," the voice replied simply. "They search for what was lost, for what was hoped for, and for what could have been."

The Unicorn inhaled deeply, stepping back from the shore. It felt a profound connection to the ocean, as though its own sorrows had long ago joined the endless waves. Yet, within that connection, it also felt a quiet determination – a strength to move forward.

"Will my journey ever end?" the Unicorn asked, its voice drifting, as lost and directionless as the mist itself.

"That depends on what YOU seek," the voice replied. "But know this – everything that is will pass. For now, keep moving forward. Someone is waiting for you."

The Unicorn turned its attention ahead, noticing a faint figure standing at the water's edge. Though distant, its presence was undeniable, a soft glow piercing through the mist.

With one last glance[077] at the ocean, the Unicorn pressed onward, stepping toward the unknown.

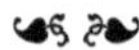

Castles in the Sand

Pride and Courage

S As the young creature continued its journey along the edge of the Ocean of Tears, the lush green grass faded into fine, golden sand that brushed against the water. Its hooves sank slightly into the soft, damp ground. The waves rolled in[045] steady, rhythmic whispers, like a quiet, unending sigh.

In the distance, against the deep blue waters, a yellow rock stood alone.

Near the shore, an old man crouched low, shaping a sandcastle with precise, deliberate movements. His long white beard swayed in the faint breeze, his hands making slow, careful moves[165] – each one a quiet reminder that every grain mattered.

"Hello there[137]," the Unicorn called softly, not wanting to disturb him. "What is your name?"

The old man looked up, his tired eyes meeting the Unicorn's. "Oh, hello – and welcome to this sandy place, my four-legged friend," he said with a gentle smile. "Once, they named[189] me Pride. But that was a long time ago." His voice trembled slightly as he pressed his hands into the sand. "And what brings you to my shore?"

"Freedom sent me," it said. "He said you might have some wisdom to share."

Pride gave a humble smile, though it didn't quite reach his eyes. "Ah, Freedom. We[192] share a similar fate, he and I. "Once, I was cherished too, held in high regard. But over time, I was set aside, overshadowed by ambition and the hunger for power. Many spoke of honouring me, but their actions told another tale."

The Unicorn stepped closer, its gaze fixed on the intricate sandcastle. "You create such beautiful things," it said earnestly. "This is the[110] most incredible sandcastle I've ever seen."

Pride chuckled softly, his hands pausing for a moment. "Thank you, my young friend. That's kind of you to say. But I've learned not to hold too tightly to what I[176] build here. The Tide of Tears will soon come and carry it away."

The Unicorn frowned, glancing at the ocean. "Then why build it at all if you know it won't last?"

Pride's eyes sparkled faintly as he resumed his work. "Because I build for the joy of creating, not for the permanence of the result. When this one is gone,

I'll simply build another – perhaps here, or maybe further down the shore," he said, gesturing briefly to the endless stretch of beach. Then, almost to himself, he mused, "Maybe I'll build two... side by side."

Watching Pride work, the Unicorn sensed something bittersweet in his dedication – both admirable and sorrowful. "Doesn't it upset you?" it asked cautiously. "Spending so much time creating, only for it to be washed away again[235]?"

Pride shook his head. "And what good would that do? Life itself is fleeting, my friend. We[126] may as well find joy in what we do while we're here."

As the two stood together, the Unicorn noticed something peculiar about the Tide of Tears. Instead of rolling in from the distant horizon, the water drifted sideways from a far-off shoreline, moving like a wide, gentle wave drawn forward[166]. It didn't crash or roar – it simply glided, silently reclaiming the sandcastle.

Stepping back, the Unicorn observed in quiet wonder as the water shifted in its peculiar rhythm. No-Place was unlike anything it had ever known. It took careful note of the ocean's shifting flow – a quiet reminder that even here, nothing followed the patterns it had come to expect, and certainty was merely an illusion.

Pride dusted the sand from his hands and turned toward the Unicorn. "Come," he said with a nod. "We'd best move on."

The two walked together, leaving the fragile sand-castle behind[012]. The Unicorn glanced back once, watching as the tide consumed the delicate structure, returning it to the formless sand.

"You didn't even look back," the Unicorn observed.

"Too busy," Pride said simply. "Too busy planning the next one."

As they walked further inland, the Unicorn noticed something unusual in the sky. Hundreds of colourful shapes floated gracefully above them, their strings anchored to the branches of a single hollow tree, standing solitary in the middle of an empty field.

"What ARE those?" it asked, gesturing toward the sky with its golden horn.

"Kites," Pride said, his voice softening. "But they're not mine – they belong to Courage. Go and meet him; he's just beyond the field. I think you'll find him interesting."

With that, Pride turned and walked back toward the shore, where the tide had just retreated. The Unicorn watched him go, feeling a strange mix of gratitude and melancholy. Then, drawn by curiosity, it turned toward the tree, eager to meet the one holding the kite's strings.

As the Unicorn approached the hollow tree, a voice called out sharply. "Don't touch the tree!"

Startled, the Unicorn stopped. "I wasn't going to!" it said defensively.

A figure stepped out from behind the tree – a tall, lean man with sharp eyes and an air of quiet intensity. His vividly colourful clothes seemed almost out of place, a stark contrast to the soft, washed-out tones of the beach. "I am Courage," he said simply, gesturing toward the kites. "And these are mine."

Courage offered a faint smile, gesturing toward the tree and the kites swaying above. He noticed the Unicorn's gaze lingering on them and spoke. "You're wondering why we're here, aren't you?" He glanced at the tree, then at the kites. "Because this tree, these strings, and the kites – they show what I am. The tree is fragile, like those who need me. The strings are the bond I offer, holding them steady but never too tight.

And the kites? They're the dreams and risks I help carry. Too much of me, and the tree snaps. "Too little, and the kites fall. But with just the right balance, they soar higher than anyone ever imagined."

The Unicorn thought for a moment, its eyes following the gentle movements of the kites and the way they tugged against their strings. "I think I see now," it said softly. "It's all about finding the right balance, isn't it?"

"Exactly," Courage said, his smile growing. "And balance is no easy thing to achieve. It takes time, effort, and sometimes even a leap of faith."

The Unicorn gazed up at the kites, their bright colours vivid against the misty sky. It felt a strange sense of awe, realising how fragile yet resilient they were. "Thank you, Courage," it said softly. "You've given me a lot to think about."

Courage nodded. "Good. Now, if you're truly seeking answers, look beyond the Canyon of Wisdom. There, you'll find the Great Wall of the Final Truth."

"The Canyon of Wisdom?" the Unicorn asked curiously.

"Yes," Courage said. "It's a place where you can ask anything, though the answers may not always be what you expect. Follow the wind, and you'll find your way."

The Unicorn once again thanked Courage, casting one last look at the kites before[074] setting off. As it walked, it felt a newfound strength within – quiet and steady, like the gentle pull of a kite string leading it onward.

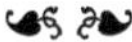

Whispers of Fate

The Wind of Destiny

T As the journey moved onward, the air grew lighter, and the mist[044] of No-Place began to shift. A soft breeze stirred – gentle at first, then strengthening with each step. It carried a whisper – low and soothing, yet undeniably commanding.

"You're on the right path."

Startled, the Unicorn paused, its golden horn catching a faint glimmer in the swirling air. "Who's there? How do you know where I'm going? And why are[160] you following me?"

The breeze curled around the Unicorn, brushing its mane and lifting its spirits ever so slightly.

"I am[173] the Wind of Destiny," the voice replied, swirling in every direction. "I do not follow you, my friend – I was here before your first step, and I will remain long after your last."

"Then how can you be so sure I'm on the right path when I don't even know where I'm going myself?"

The wind swirled playfully around its hooves, carrying faint whispers of laughter. "You're on the right path," Destiny replied, "because you chose to take it. Every step forward brings you closer to something new, even if what lies ahead remains_unseen."

The Unicorn tilted its head slightly, doubt flickering in its gaze. "But what if I've chosen the wrong path? What if another way would have been better?"

The wind stirred, lifting the young creature's mane in a reassuring embrace. "There is no wrong path," it said, its voice flowing like a melody carried through time. "There is only the one you choose to walk. Your steps shape the[209] journey, and every choice brings you closer to understanding. You worry too much, my young friend."

"I suppose..." the Unicorn admitted, its gaze drifting toward the distant horizon. "But it's hard to feel certain about anything here."

"That is the nature of existence," Destiny explained, its tone softer now, like the gentle rustling of leaves on a quiet autumn day. "Certainty is a rare thing in life. Trust in your heart and the journey you've chosen. I am here to[113] guide, not to decide – that is your gift alone."

The Unicorn's hooves tapped lightly against the ground as it considered these words. "You're saying the choices I make shape the path I walk?"

"Exactly," Destiny replied, its voice now swirling like a quiet storm. "The path and your[075] choices are intertwined – one cannot exist without the other. Isn't it foolish to believe the path shapes us without realising that our steps shape the path just as much? Tell me, have you ever wondered what comes first – the silence around you or the quiet you carry inside...?"

Destiny's voice softened. "But remember this: your path is yours alone. Many lose their way by following the wrong turns of others. Listen to your heart and follow your instinct – they always know the[013] way and where you truly belong."

The breeze danced around the young creature once more, brushing past its horn and gently urging it forward. The Unicorn stepped lightly, a quiet strength settling in its chest. And though it did not yet know where the path would lead, for the first time[140], it no longer felt the need to.

❦

Shattered Spirit

Splinters of the Spirit of Man

S The Unicorn nodded, its determination growing stronger. The wind's gentle push became a guiding nudge, parting the mist to reveal something startling in the distance – a towering heap of coloured, shattered glass[039]. The shards glittered like tiny stars, their jagged edges catching the faint LIGHT in a chaotic, glimmering display.

"What is that?" the Unicorn asked, stopping to stare, its voice woven with awe and unease.

"That," Destiny said softly, its tone almost reverent, "is the Spirit of Man."

Watching the fractured mound shimmer in the distance, the Unicorn stepped forward, its movements slow and deliberate. With every stride, the heap loomed larger, its presence bearing down like an unspoken weight. The mist curled around its hooves as the sharp scent of something old – dust and time[238] – filled the air.

As it neared, scattered fragments crunched beneath its hooves. At the foot of the heap, something caught its eye – an old pot of glue, its edges crusted with dried residue, once used but long abandoned.

"The Spirit of Man?" it echoed. "Why does it look so... broken?"

Destiny's voice lowered, as though sharing a burden too heavy to carry. "It is shattered under the weight of its own contradictions – strength and fragility, hope and despair, love and fear. Yet, even in pieces, it glimmers. There[078] is beauty to be found even in its brokenness."

The Unicorn gazed into the jagged pile. Within THE shards, it thought it glimpsed fleeting images: faces filled with laughter and tears, hands building and destroying, moments of triumph and despair.

"Why doesn't anyone put it back together?"

Destiny sighed, the breeze softening into a quiet whisper of sorrow. "Many have tried, but the Spirit of Man is not[015] something one can mend alone. It is shaped by every choice, every action. Only when enough hearts move together can it begin to heal."

As the Unicorn lowered its head, its golden horn caught a faint reflection in one of the larger shards. For a moment, it saw itself – surrounded by both light and shadow.

"I[055] don't understand," it said. "It's broken... because of all of us[168]?"

"Yes, it is," Destiny replied. "But it is also whole because of us. Every piece tells a story – of struggle, of resilience, of the power to rise even when broken. That is the paradox of the Spirit of Man: fragile, yet resilient."

The Unicorn stepped back and suddenly realised that what is right is simply what remains after we have done everything wrong. Its heart felt both heavy and inspired. "How can I help repair it?" it asked, its voice trembling with both doubt and hope.

Destiny's voice grew tender. "It all begins with a single piece. Many see the task as impossible because they focus only on the whole, overwhelmed by its brokenness. But even a single shard, placed with care, can begin to strengthen it."

When its gaze settled[108] on two shards near its hooves, it noticed their jagged edges seemed to align, as if they had once belonged together. Slowly, it picked them up, careful not to cut itself, and placed them side by side. With deliberate precision, it dipped the tip of its hoof into the sticky, ageing glue and pressed the pieces together. The shards shimmered softly, their connection delicate yet infused with newfound strength.

"Look! I did it!" the Unicorn exclaimed, a shimmer of pride in its voice.

Destiny's tone softened, carrying quiet warmth. "You see? It's not your task to finish the work, only to begin it – or[200] at least to contribute. Imagine if everyone placed just one piece... how much could be restored?"

The Unicorn smiled faintly and continued its work, carefully selecting fragments that seemed to match. Though its progress was slow and the pile immense, it felt as if it were assembling a vast puzzle – each shard placed with care and intention. It knew it could never restore the Spirit of Man alone, for it was[138] never meant to be mended by one. But each connection felt like a small victory, a step toward something whole.

Suddenly a faint light stirred deep within the pile. At first, it was barely noticeable – a flicker, like the last spark of a dying fire. But with every shard restored, the light grew stronger. Then, a tiny golden sparkle emerged, hovering delicately above the fragments. Its glow pulsed softly, brightening with each repaired piece.

"Hope!" the Unicorn called out, its voice bright with excitement and recognition.

The sparkle swirled upward, casting a soft, golden glow over the shattered pile. Destiny's voice returned, steady and_reassuring. "Go! Follow Hope. The NEXT chapter of your journey awaits."

The Unicorn hesitated, glancing back at the scattered shards. The task was far from complete, yet the glow of Hope filled its heart with renewed strength. "I'll return," it said under its breath, as though speaking to the broken pieces – or perhaps to itself. "I promise I will come back."

"Good," Destiny said, its voice dissolving into the breeze. "Now, follow the path ahead. The Canyon of Wisdom awaits."

As the Unicorn turned to follow the golden glow, it carried within its heart the shimmering reflections of the Spirit of Man –broken yet beautiful, fragile yet enduring.

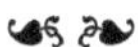

Fragments of Who We Were

Forgotten Memories

O The journey led the young traveller to an awe-inspiring sight – a vast, towering shelf stretching endlessly into the misty void of No-Place. It groaned under the weight of countless books, their spines worn and faded with age. The air carried the faint scent of paper and ink, laced with a quiet sorrow, as if the stories themselves longed to be heard.

Stepping closer, it spotted an old woman standing before the shelf. She was frail yet moved with quiet purpose, her hands gracefully sorting through the books. Though her back was slightly bent, her eyes sparkled with an intensity that defied her years.

"Forgive me for interrupting," the Unicorn said politely, lowering its head in respect. "May I[079] ask who you are and why you keep all these books?"

The old woman turned slowly, her gaze meeting the Unicorn's with a kind, knowing smile. "I am the Librarian of Forgotten Memories," she said, her voice steady and gentle. "These books hold memories –

fragments of lives once lived, moments lost to time or willingly left behind."

Gazing up at the towering shelves, the Unicorn felt overwhelmed by their sheer scale. "There are so many," it said softly, the enormity of the place pressing heavily against its chest.

"Indeed," the Librarian replied, her tone a mix of sorrow and pride. "Each book is a fragment of someone's story – a piece of their self. Some memories were abandoned willingly, too painful, too heavy, too inconvenient to carry. Others slipped away so quietly, lost to time and neglect."

As the Unicorn moved closer, its hoof brushed against a small, dusty, dark red book lying on the ground. It nudged the book gently, almost as if afraid it might crumble. "What happens to these memories if they're forgotten?" it asked, its golden horn catching the[046] faint light filtering through the mist.

"They fade," the Librarian said, her voice soft with regret. "But they never truly disappear. They linger here, waiting for someone to remember them. Memories shape who we are, and without them, we lose pieces of ourselves[232]. We become... unwhole."

The young traveller thought of those it had encountered back home – of how Love, Honesty, and Freedom had been forgotten. "Can these memories ever find their way back?" it asked, a flicker of hope brightening its voice. "Or will they simply fade, lost without the ones who once held them?"

The Librarian's expression was serious yet kind. "They can be reunited, but[203] only if they are sought out. Memories cannot be forced upon anyone. They must be chosen – chosen by those willing to face what was once lost."

The Unicorn carefully picked up the small red book, then placed it gently before the Librarian. "Here," it said, nudging it forward. "This one looks like it's waiting for someone."

The Librarian accepted the book with a warm smile, cradling it as though it were something precious. "You have a kind heart. Perhaps, one day, those who have forgotten will find their way back – to these memories, to themselves, and maybe even to you."

Gazing up at the towering shelf one last time, its heart heavy yet hopeful. Each book seemed to whisper, calling for someone to turn its pages, to breathe life into the stories held within. With a deep breath, it turned to leave.

But something was... not quite right.

A single book sat slightly askew on the shelf – its spine unmarked, its presence unnatural, like a note left behind in a dream. The Unicorn hesitated. It wasn't sure why it had noticed this book among thousands, but something about it felt... misplaced.

It stepped closer, brushing away the thin layer of DUST. As its horn touched the cover, the faintest outline of letters stirred beneath the surface.

A name? A title?

The ink swirled, shifting as though alive, forming words that hovered just on the edge of meaning. But the moment the Unicorn tried[086] to read them, they faded – gone, as if they had never been there at all.

The Librarian paused beside it, her gaze fixed on the book with quiet thoughtfulness. Her fingers hovered just above the cover, but she did not touch it.

"Curious..." she murmured, her expression unreadable. Then, after a moment, she shook her head and walked on, as if the moment had already slipped from memory.

The Unicorn lingered a heartbeat longer before turning away.

"Wait," the Librarian's voice cut through the stillness of the endless shelves – soft but deliberate.

It froze mid-step, anticipation threading through its thoughts like an unseen current. Slowly, it turned, its golden horn catching the dusty light as it met the Librarian's steady gaze once more.

"These memories are fragments of a forgotten time. But if you seek to mend what is broken or find what is lost, YOU must seek the Weaver of Time," she said, her tone firm yet kind. "The Weaver resides beyond[016] the Great Wall of the Final Truth. Only the Weaver can weave these forgotten pieces back into something whole."

The Unicorn's eyes widened as the weight of her words settled. It stood silently for a moment, then lifted its head with steady determination, ready to continue its journey.

"The path will reveal itself," the Librarian said gently. "Trust your heart, and let it guide you. But be warned: the journey is not easy. The Weaver will not simply hand you the answers. You must show them why these memories matter."

The Unicorn nodded, its purpose becoming[136] clearer. "I'll find them. I'll help them reclaim what was lost."

The Librarian's smile was faint but hopeful. "Then you already carry the spark of what is needed. Go now, and may your memories light your way."

Before stepping away, the Unicorn whispered a quiet promise to the silent rows of books. "I'll remind them. I'll help them remember."

As it walked on, the scent of ink and paper lingered in the air – a bittersweet reminder of what had been forgotten, and what could still be found.

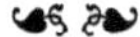

Echoes of Belonging

A Glimmer of Home

N The path grew quieter, and the mist of No-Place softened, like a protective whisper. Memories of the world[144] left behind crept into the Unicorn's mind – the vibrant forest painted in colour, the gentle warmth of the sun, and the laughter of children who had once believed in its magic.

It paused, gazing upward into the empty, endless sky. "I miss it," the Unicorn said softly. "I miss the forest, the flowers, and those who once believed in me."

Destiny swirled around softly, its voice gentle yet searching. "What is it you miss, Little One – the place itself, or their belief in you that[148] gave it life?"

The Unicorn lowered its head, its golden horn reflecting faintly in the soft, diffused light. "Both, I think," it said thoughtfully. "The belief made the forest feel alive, like it was part of me. Without it, I don't know who I am."

Destiny's voice softened, brushing against the Unicorn like a comforting breeze. "The belief of others does[103] not define you. Your magic comes from within. The forest was not your home because they believed – it was your home because it was where you belonged. Home is not a place; it is a feeling – a connection to something greater, a sense of belonging."

The Unicorn stood still, the words resonating deeply. It thought of the faint memories it still held of the world it[017] had left behind – the quiet belief that something greater remained, even if it was hidden or forgotten.

"I know it's still there," the Unicorn said, a quiet certainty rising within. "Distant, but not gone."

"Then your home is never truly lost," Destiny replied, its voice flowing like a distant melody. "A forest does not vanish just because it is unseen. No-Place reflects the hearts of those who once believed, and as long as even a whisper of it remains, there is always a way back. It may not be as it was, but it can still be found – if you choose to seek it."

As it raised its head, the weight of loneliness began[080] to ease. "Maybe I can help bring back what was forgotten?" it said, its voice growing steadier. "If I can remind the world of Love, Honesty, and all the others... maybe belief will return. Maybe... even I will be seen again."

Destiny's presence deepened slightly, a warm breeze stirring the Unicorn's shimmering mane. It hesitated, the wind shifting ever so slightly – as[204] if uncertain. "You carry the spark of possibility – a powerful gift." The words were gentle, carefully chosen, like a soft tale meant to comfort rather than to promise. "Hold on to it, and you may yet find your way home."

The Unicorn closed its eyes to see more clearly, drawing in a deep breath. In that stillness, it sensed the faint pulse of[179] connection – a thread weaving between the world it had left behind and the journey that lay ahead. When it opened its eyes again, the path ahead seemed clearer. The mist, though still present, felt lighter – as if something unspoken had finally settled.

In the distance, the silhouette of a young man appeared – too far to call out to, yet impossible to ignore. For a brief moment, it seemed like Honesty – waving, signalling – but as quickly as it had appeared, it was gone.

With renewed determination, it turned back toward the winding road. In its heart, it carried the memories of what was and the hope of what could be – a quiet truth, a promise waiting to be fulfilled.

Home was never a place to return to. It was something to hold close. Something to rebuild, whenever needed. To find what was lost, you must walk forward. To stay true to yourself, you must dare to leave.

And so, it continued its journey.

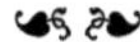

A Last Drop of Innocence

The Pure Lake and the Fountain of Innocence

L After a walk that felt both brief and endless, the mist began to thin, revealing a grand fountain that seemed to emerge from the silence[047] itself. Once majestic, its structure was now crumbling – the stone cracked and weathered, its elaborately carved spouts long dry. A barren, dust-filled basin surrounded it, its emptiness stark against the misty void of No-Place. Inscribed faintly on its surface were the words:

'The Fountain of Innocence'

Before the Unicorn could approach the fountain, a wet squish echoed beneath its hooves, startling it. Looking down, it saw its legs submerged in thick, murky water. It leapt back, the foul-smelling mud clinging stubbornly to its white coat.

"Hey, you! Be careful! Don't come any closer! You'll drown in me!"

The Unicorn blinked[073] in surprise. "Who's there? Who said that?" it asked, scanning its surroundings. Then it realised – the voice was coming from the muddy pool itself.

"I am the Pure Lake," the voice replied, deep and echoing, as if rising from unseen depths.

"You don't look very pure to me – if you don't mind me saying so," the Unicorn remarked, wrinkling its nose at the stench.

The lake chuckled, a sound like ripples spreading across its surface. "Don't be fooled by appearances, young traveller. I am called the Pure Lake not because my waters ARE clear, but because I reflect the truth. What you see is not my impurity – it is the reflection of the world as it has been shaped[142]."

Stepping back to avoid the muddy edge, the Unicorn frowned. "What do you mean? This is just... mud."

The lake's voice softened, almost pitying the Unicorn's innocence. "I am a mirror, my young friend. My waters reflect the world – not as it wishes to be seen, but as it truly is. If I appear muddy and foul, it is because hearts are heavy, thoughts are clouded, and innocence has been tarnished. Do you understand now?"

The Unicorn stared at the lake, its golden horn dimming slightly. "Then... is this what lies within?"

"Yes," the lake replied. "But you mustn't let it dishearten you. Even the murkiest waters can be cleared. Change begins with those who dare to see the truth. Perhaps[228], in time, you will help bring clarity to clouded eyes – so their reflections can shine again."

As it pondered these words, it carefully stepped away from the muddy edge, its gaze shifting toward the silent, empty fountain nearby. "Maybe I could wash off in the Fountain."

A low laugh bubbled from the Pure Lake. "Oh, you poor thing! You didn't think the fountain was still filled with clear water, did you? It dried up long ago. No one comes here to cleanse their innocence anymore, so the water slowly vanished, leaving only dust and stone. But if you insist[105] on cleaning your legs, there's a patch of clear water near the purple rock on my far side."

The Unicorn hesitated, glancing between the dusty fountain and the muddy lake. Finally, it sighed and made its way around the lake to the purple rock. Sitting down carefully, it found a small pool of relatively clear water and began scrubbing the mud from its legs.

"Why did they stop coming to the fountain?" the Unicorn asked, glancing over its shoulder at the dried basin.

"Its value was forgotten," the Pure Lake replied simply. "Innocence, once cherished, became something to hide, something to mock – dismissed as naive, as childish. Greed, pride, and deceit seeped into too many hearts, and the fountain could no longer sustain itself. Innocence, once lost, cannot be reclaimed – but[018] it can be protected, nurtured in those who still carry it. That is how the fountain may one day flow again."

With its legs cleansed, the Unicorn's gaze lingered on the empty fountain. "I'm searching for the Great Wall of the Final Truth," it said. "I need to reach the Weaver of Time and ask for guidance. Can you show me the way?"

The Pure Lake rippled faintly, its voice laced with regret. "I would, if my waters were clear. But as you see, they are muddied with the weight of the world. I can only offer this: the Great Wall lies beyond the Desert of Endless Knowledge. But beware, young traveller – it is a treacherous place, and only those who stand firm in their purpose can withstand its trials."

The Unicorn nodded, its confidence growing. "Thank you," it said softly. "I may not[174] see the path ahead, but your words have offered me a different kind of direction."

The Pure Lake chuckled, its tone lightening. "Be careful, Little Unicorn. Even truth, when reflected too clearly, can be as overwhelming as a revealed lie. Travel safely, and may you always find what you seek."

About to continue its journey, it neared the fountain – when a voice, flat and unimpressed, echoed through the empty space. "You've come looking for something, haven't you?"

Startled, the Unicorn turned toward the dry pool. Within it stood a faint, shimmering figure – more reflection than form, vague and indistinct, as though only half-there.

"You have reached the Fountain of Innocence," the voice continued. "But I'm afraid what you seek is not here. Though, deep down, you already knew that."

"Who am I speaking to?" the Little Unicorn asked, cautious but intrigued.

"I am the guardian of this fountain," the voice replied, growing clearer as the figure shifted. "Or, what remains of it. Once, its waters flowed freely – pure and abundant. It was a place where those who had lost themselves came to remember, to cleanse their hearts of guilt, fear, and regret. But now..." The guardian gestured toward the empty basin. "Without innocence, there is nothing left to renew."

The Unicorn lowered its head, feeling a wave of sadness. "Is there no way to bring the water back?"

The guardian hesitated, its form flickering like a fading, colourless flame. "Perhaps," it said softly. "The Pure Lake reflects what is, but this fountain is different – it responds to what could be. If the world remembers how to see with pure eyes – to act with kindness, honesty, and compassion – then, maybe, the waters will return."

Staring into the dry basin, the Unicorn stood silently for a moment[206]. "I'll try," it said, lifting its head. "I'll remind the world of what has been forgotten. Maybe – just maybe – someone will hear me."

The guardian's form brightened faintly, a glimmer of hope sparking within its translucent figure. "Even the smallest trace of innocence can grow if nurtured."

The Unicorn nodded quietly, a newfound determination settling within. As it turned to leave, a faint shimmer caught its eye at the edge of the fountain – a single droplet of water, clinging stubbornly to the stone. It wasn't much, but it was something – and that was a start.

Where Silence Answers

The Canyon of Wisdom

Y Following the faint glow ahead, the Little Unicorn reached the edge of a vast abyss. A strange luminescence pulsed from deep within[019] the canyon, casting shifting patterns along its sheer cliffs.

The void stretched endlessly in both directions, its cliffs plunging into a void so deep that no bottom could be seen. The air here felt heavy, as though every word spoken would ripple through time itself.

A familiar warmth stirred beside the Unicorn. As it turned, it saw Hope hovering nearby, her glow steady and reassuring.

"This is the Canyon of Wisdom," Hope explained. "Here, you may ask anything that troubles you, and the echoes will lead you to the answers you seek."

Carefully the Unicorn stepped closer to the edge, peering into the endless depths. "How does it work?" it asked.

"Speak[231] your question aloud," Hope said, her golden light flickering softly. "But be prepared – wisdom has a habit of speaking in riddles."

Taking a deep breath, the Little Unicorn raised its head and called into the canyon. "HELLO? CAN YOU HEAR ME?"

The words echoed back: "...HEAR ME ...Hear me ...me." The words weren't rehearsed[118]. They simply came, because they needed to.

Startled by its own voice, the Unicorn hesitated before trying again. "I NEED SOMEONE TO BELIEVE IN ME!"

The canyon repeated the plea: "...BELIEVE IN ME ...Believe in me ...in me."

The repetition felt[049] strange, as though the words were not merely echoes, but reflections. The Unicorn's breath caught as it realised the canyon wasn't offering answers – it was holding up a mirror. The wisdom here was not in the responses, but in the questions themselves.

"I don't think I understand," the Unicorn said quietly, stepping back from the edge.

"You're beginning to," Hope said softly. "The echoes don't give answers – they reveal the questions you already carry. Keep asking, and listen[225] closely. Not with your ears, but with your heart."

"I've walked this far, and still, I wonder: Who am I WAITING for? What am I hoping to find? I tell myself I am searching for something – someone – but deep down, I know the truth, don't I? It has always been me. I was the one who needed to believe."

"I was the one who needed to remember."

"I was the one who had to step forward."

"And if that is true for me... then maybe, just maybe, it is true FOR you too?"

Gathering its courage, the Unicorn stepped forward again. "WHAT IS MY PURPOSE?" it called out.

The canyon responded:" ...MY PURPOSE ...Purpose ...purpose."

"WHY DO I FEEL SO LOST?" the Unicorn asked, its voice trembling.

"...SO LOST ...Lost ...lost."

As it listened to the echoes fading into the abyss, the Unicorn noticed that each question felt heavier than the last, yet no clear answers came. But perhaps that was the lesson – wisdom was not in the answers themselves, but in understanding why the questions existed at all.

"Wisdom?" came a sneering voice from[082] behind. "Is that what you think you'll find here?"

The Unicorn spun around, startled, to see the Shadow of Doubt materialising from the mist at the edges of the canyon. Its form twisted and shimmered, never settling into one shape, as though caught between existence and nothingness. Shadows of darkness coiled around it, reaching out like whispers of fear.

"You think you've gained insight," the Shadow said, its voice smooth but oozing with arrogance. "But all you've done is listen to your own voice. Wisdom doesn't change reality[164] – it doesn't make you less alone."

Taking A step back, the young creature's horn shimmered a little less brightly. "I don't need it to change reality[096]," it said, though its voice trembled. "Wisdom changes how I see the path ahead."

The Shadow laughed, sharp and cold, like glass shattering in an empty room. Its form surged forward, expanding briefly before collapsing into a twisting silhouette. "And what good is that?" it hissed. "You're still alone, wandering a place where belief holds no power. Who will follow a symbol long forgotten? Who will care if you fail?"

The Unicorn's chest tightened, the weight of the Shadow's words pressing heavily against its spirit. But then it closed its eyes, focusing on the faint connection deep within – a glowing pulse of strength, steady despite the warm chill of the canyon. Hope's gentle light flickered beside it, a silent reminder of the strength it carried within.

It opened its eyes and stood tall. "I may be a symbol," it said confidently, its golden horn glowing softly, pushing back the mist. "But I carry the strength of everyone I've met – and that's enough to keep me going."

For a brief moment, the Shadow hesitated, its shifting form flickering as though caught in its own conflict. Its sharp edges softened, its darkness dimmed, and it mumbled quietly, as if speaking to itself. Then, without another word, it dissolved into the mist, leaving behind a faint chill – like a whisper of doubt that refused to fully fade.

With the Shadow's disappearance, the mist around the canyon began to shift. The Unicorn let out a shaky breath, turning back to the path ahead, feeling the quiet warmth of Hope beside it. Though the Shadow's words still echoed faintly in its mind, its spirit burned brighter.

"I'm not alone," it whispered, its voice steady.

Turning back to the canyon, it drew a deep breath and called out, louder this time: "WHY SHOULD I BELIEVE IN MYSELF?"

The canyon answered, its echo[202] returning softer now, almost like a knowing whisper: "...BELIEVE IN MYSELF ...Believe in myself ...myself."

Standing in silence, the Unicorn listened to the fading echoes. Slowly, understanding settled in – the canyon was not a place of answers, but a mirror, reflecting the questions it needed to face.

"Do you see now?" Hope asked gently, drifting closer, her glow like the first light of dawn. "The answers don't come from out there. They come from within."

The Unicorn nodded, a quiet understanding settling in. "The canyon doesn't give answers," it whispered, more to the wind than to anyone else. "It only shows me where to look for them."

"That's correct," Hope said, her voice calm and reassuring. "True wisdom isn't found in the words of others, but in first asking yourself the right questions."

"I've been searching so hard," the young traveller said. "Maybe I've been looking in the wrong places all along. Perhaps everything I needed was inside me – just waiting to be seen."

Hope hovered beside it, her glow steady. "That realisation is the first step toward understanding," she said softly. "The answers you seek will come when the time is right. Trust the questions, Little Unicorn, and trust your journey – those are your truest guides."

Standing taller, the Unicorn's eyes flickered with newfound clarity. Across the canyon, a faint shimmer of light emerged on the horizon.

"What comes next?" it asked, its voice steady and determined.

Hope gestured toward the distant glow. "Beyond the canyon lies the Great Wall of the Final Truth. But first, you must cross the Silver Cord and travel through the Desert of Endless Knowledge. The path will not be easy."

"I'll keep going," the Unicorn said with confidence.

"Some things are too quiet to recall, yet they echo anyway," it wondered, and with one last glance at the

Canyon of Wisdom, it turned from the edge and continued its journey, Hope casting a gentle light ahead. Behind it, the echoes lingered – not as answers, but as reminders of the questions still waiting to be understood.

A Bridge of Light

Silver Cord

A The Little Unicorn followed Hope's guiding light until the air around it shimmered with a pulse of energy unlike anything it had encountered before. The ground beneath its hooves felt firm yet weightless, as though it were treading on something beyond the tangible. Ahead, a radiant glowing thread stretched infinitely in both directions, connecting the visible world[111] to something unseen.

With its eyes fixed on the glistening strand of light, the Unicorn asked quietly, "Is this the Silver Cord?" Its voice was barely above a[021] whisper.

"It is," Hope_replied softly, her glow steady. "It is the lifeline of existence, an eternal web that connects all things. It binds every heart to its dreams, to its emotions, to Love, Honesty, and Freedom. But it also stretches beyond, weaving through time and space, linking one moment to the next, one soul to another."

Marvelling at how the cord seemed alive, vibrating with a rhythm that resonated deep within, the young traveller stepped closer. "It's unlike anything I've ever seen. But why can't I see where it begins?"

"Because it has neither BEGINNING nor end," Hope explained. "The Silver Cord is infinite, existing beyond the limits of the physical world. It connects all things – to each other and to something greater – forming an unbroken web of existence."

As the Unicorn gazed, it noticed delicate threads branching from[182] the cord, stretching toward faint, glowing figures in the distance. "Those threads," it thought aloud, "they connect to everything – even to Love, Honesty, and all the way up the mountain to Freedom."

Hope hovered beside. "Yes. Each is woven into this great connection, just as you are. The cord runs through every soul, linking one to another – reaching even those who have yet to recognise it."

"Then... I'm part of it[051] too?" the Unicorn asked hesitantly, a strange feeling stirring within.

"Of course," Hope replied. "Look closely, and you'll see."

Peering at the cord, it noticed a faint thread of light extending from its golden horn, merging seamlessly with the[083] shimmering web. The connection felt warm and steady, a quiet reminder that it was part of something far greater than itself.

"I can feel it," the Unicorn said, wonder filling its voice. "I can see it. It's as if... I am part of something infinite."

Hope circled around the golden horn, her light brightening as if to embrace it. "You are," she said warmly. "This connection isn't just a reminder of who you are – it's a reminder of who you've always been. Let it guide you forward and remind you that you are never truly alone – not even in the darkest of times."

The Unicorn lifted its head, the pulse of the Silver Cord seemingly aligning with the steady rhythm of its heart. "It's part of me," it realised, its will strengthening. It gazed at the endless web of light, its heart swelling with a[146] mix of awe and gratitude. "Does everyone share this[237] connection?" it asked.

"Yes," Hope replied, her glow intensifying. "BUT it is often forgotten. The noise of the world drowns out the gentle pull of the cord, and so many drift – unaware of the connection still woven within them."

She paused, her voice gentle yet resolute. "Remember – some things can only be seen once they are believed."

A newfound awareness slowly settled within the young creature. "Then I'll stay mindful of my connection. And I'll try to help others remember theirs, too."

Hope's light brightened in response. "That is a noble purpose, my friend. Remember, as long as you feel the Silver Cord, you can never lose your way."

The Unicorn gazed at the shimmering thread one last time, its light fading into the misty horizon. Each vibration held a quiet promise, a silent whisper rippling through existence itself.

With a deep breath, it turned and continued its journey. Behind[213] it, the Silver Cord pulsed faintly – a quiet assurance of belonging and connection. Though the path ahead remained shrouded in mystery, the Unicorn carried the comfort of the cord's unbreakable bond, knowing it was part of something infinite.

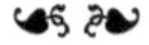

Storm in the Stillness

The Clouds of Thoughts

S As the young traveller ventured deeper into No-Place, its gaze lifted. Above, immense clouds floated in the vast sky, their forms ever-shifting in shape and colour. They drifted freely, unbound by gravity or rules, painting the heavens with[150] their vivid, living presence.

The Unicorn's eyes widened as it watched them swirl and change. "They're different from any clouds I've seen before... What are they?"

"Those are the Clouds of Thoughts," Hope explained, glowing steadily beside the Unicorn. "They drift between worlds, unrestrained by boundaries. They are echoes of ideas, waiting to be[114] shaped into something real."

Each cloud was unique – some shimmering with light, others soft and pastel, their edges glowing faintly. They moved gracefully, weaving through one another like[020] dancers in a silent waltz. "They're so vibrant and alive," the Unicorn marvelled.

"Yes," Hope agreed. "But look closer."

Soon, it noticed darker clouds tangled among the vibrant ones. They swirled and clashed, their forms sharp and turbulent, disturbing the harmony of the brighter ones.

"Why do some look so... unsettled?" the Unicorn asked, its voice softening.

"Not ALL thoughts are kind or[214] constructive," Hope explained. "Some are filled with fear, anger, and envy. These thoughts twist the brighter ones, creating storms that ripple through everything."

The Unicorn's heart sank as it watched a vibrant pink cloud consumed by a shadowy one, the two merging into a swirling, chaotic storm drained of all colour. Flashes of light flickered within, struggling against the darkness before being[234] swallowed whole.

"Can they be calmed?" the Unicorn asked, looking at Hope.

"Only by those who create them," Hope said. "Thoughts are powerful – they can shape worlds, build dreams, or destroy them. The skies will always hold these clouds, but when thoughts are nurtured with care, light will outnumber the darkness."

The gentle traveller watched as a colourful cloud, faint and flickering, broke free from the storm. It floated higher, shimmering softly as it drifted toward the clearer sky. "It's not[087] lost. Not yet," the Unicorn said firmly.

"No, not all," Hope replied. "But the balance is fragile. When kind thoughts are nurtured, they grow and shine, keeping the storms at bay. Yet this wisdom has faded, and so the skies have grown restless."

The Unicorn's gaze lingered on the chaotic scene above, the interplay of light and shadow casting a shifting pattern on the ground. A flicker of determination lit its eyes. "Then I'll remind them of this too," it said firmly. "Maybe they've just forgotten how much their thoughts really matter."

Hope's glow brightened softly, as though in silent agreement. The Unicorn raised its head, its golden horn gleaming faintly as it walked on, leaving the shifting sky behind. Above them, the clouds continued their eternal dance – some serene, others restless – but the young traveller carried the quiet promise that even the wildest storms will one day calm.

⋆⋅☆⋅⋆

Chains of Desire

Violence & the Twins Envy and Greed

W The path ahead grew darker, the air heavier, thick with hostility. In the distance, three figures loomed, standing imposingly in the middle of the road. As the Little Unicorn approached, it noticed[115] that two of them were nearly[127] identical, their forms twisted and hunched. Their faces were hollow, with dark pits where their eyes should have been. The third figure was larger and more imposing, his body cracked and glowing faintly with a dark light from within.

The smaller figures turned toward the innocent creature, their gazes filled with amusement.

The first, thin and skeletal, moved with sharp, erratic gestures, his grin stretching too wide. "Look at this one," he sneered, his voice like[050] a blade scraping ice. "So pure, so untainted. Do YOU think you're better than us?" He straightened, his hollow eyes gleaming. "I am Envy."

The second figure let out a slow, rattling chuckle. Bloated and draped in glittering chains, jewels, and ornaments, he ran a hand over his treasures, letting them clink together like whispered temptations. "Ah, but I suppose you don't care for such things, do you?" he mused, his voice dripping with false charm. "How noble. How dull." His empty grin widened. "I am Greed."

The largest figure stepped forward, his scarred, fractured form carrying an air of unspoken malice. A low, jagged laugh scraped from deep within his chest. "And I," he growled, towering over the Unicorn, "am Violence. I don't ask. I take."

His deep voice echoed through the mist, unsettling it like distant thunder. "And whatever they desire, I deliver."

The Unicorn instinctively stepped back, its heart racing. A dark energy surrounded the trio, thick like a suffocating fog[014]. "What do you want from me?" it asked cautiously.

Envy raised a bony finger, pointing straight at the Unicorn's shimmering horn. "That," he spat. "Your horn. It's too bright. I can't stand that it's yours and not mine."

Greed nodded, his empty eyes glinting with cruel hunger. "Me too! I want it too," he added, his voice thick with longing. "Not because I need it, but because if I SEE something, I must have it."

The Unicorn's chest tightened. "But my horn is part of me!" it protested. "I can't give it to you[212]!"

"That doesn't matter," Violence growled, his fists clenching tightly, the cracks on his body glowing brighter. "If they want it, I'll take it."

Though fear twisted in its chest, the Unicorn stood its ground. "Why do you want it so badly? What would you even do with it?"

Envy smirked, his hollow eyes narrowing. "It's not about what I'll do with it. It's about you not having it. If I can't have it, then no one should."

Greed let out a low chuckle, his tone slick and mocking. "For me, it's simple: I want everything[183]. I want to have it, own it, hoard it, and make sure no one else ever touches it."

Violence stepped forward, the ground trembling faintly beneath his weight. "Enough talk," he snarled. "If they want it, I will take it. Now."

Desperation surged in the Unicorn's heart. "Destiny! Help me!" it cried. But the air remained silent; no guiding voice answered. Its golden horn dimmed as the truth settled in – it was on its own.

The Unicorn spun and_fled, its hooves pounding against the ground as fast as they could carry it. Behind, Violence thundered forward, his massive form charging with terrifying force. But his speed hindered – the heavy chains binding him to Envy and Greed held him back.

Envy clawed at the ground, his skeletal frame shuddering with frustration, while Greed clung desperately to his glittering trophies, unwilling to let them go.

The fearless creature ran until the trio's cries and growls faded into the distance. At last, it stopped, its sides heaving as it caught its breath. When it turned back, it saw the three figures struggling against their own chains, bound by the weight of their own desires.

"They're so hopelessly lost," the Unicorn said, its voice heavy with sadness. "They don't even recognise the beauty in what they already have."

"And that is why they will[240] never be free," Hope's steady voice sounded, reappearing beside the young explorer. "They can never be satisfied. Their chains are of their own making."

For a moment longer, the Unicorn watched the trio from a safe distance, a newfound understanding settling in its heart. "I won't let them control me," it said firmly. "I'll cherish what is mine, respect what is not, and keep moving forward."

Hope's light brightened in quiet agreement. "That is the key to resisting them – gratitude and self-awareness. Those who see their own worth have no need for Envy, Greed, or Violence. Sometimes, wanting less allows you to have more."

As the Unicorn turned back toward the path ahead, its golden horn cast a steady glow into the darkness. With every step, its determination grew, and the chains that had once weighed on its heart faded like distant memories[084]. Looking back one last time, it saw the trio still struggling, bound not by force, but by their own refusal to let go.

It vowed to carry this lesson forward – a reminder that true strength isn't about taking or possessing, but about knowing when to release, when to move on, and when to trust what already lies within.

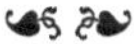

The Price of Letting Go

Sacrifice

Further along the path, the Little Unicorn noticed something gleaming in the dust – a golden ring, polished and unblemished, its surface catching the[215] faint light of No-Place. Puzzled, it was drawn to its quiet beauty and the mystery of why such a precious object had been left behind.

It stepped four steps closer, leaning down to examine it. Just as it reached out with its golden horn, a voice spoke, steady and calm.

"Are you sure you want to take that?"

Startled, the Unicorn looked around but saw no one. "Who's there?" it asked, its voice cautious and uncertain.

"I am Sacrifice," came the reply, resonating softly from the[153] air around the ring. "And I must ask – why do you want the ring?"

Its gaze lingering on the object, the Unicorn replied, "It's beautiful, and it looks abandoned. Maybe I could keep it or give it to someone who might want it."

Sacrifice's tone grew thoughtful. "It is tempting, isn't it? But consider this – the ring was lost, not discarded. It carries the mourning of loss, and taking it might mean robbing someone of the chance to reclaim what was once theirs."

The Unicorn frowned, looking down at the gleaming object. "But what if they never come back? What if someone else takes it instead?"

"That may happen," Sacrifice admitted. "But what others choose to do does not diminish the value of your[053] own actions. Sacrifice is not about controlling outcomes – it's about doing what feels true to you. Sometimes, it means letting go of something you desire for THE sake of what is right."

The air swirled restlessly around the Unicorn's hooves. "Look down – this ring doesn't even fit you[085], yet you still hesitate to let it go."

The Unicorn pondered these words, tilting its head as it considered the ring's fate. After a moment, it bent down and picked it up carefully. "If I leave it here, it might go unnoticed. But if I place it somewhere more visible..."

With deliberate care, it placed the ring on a nearby rock, its golden surface catching the dim glow of No-

Place's light. "This way, if the owner comes searching, they'll have a better chance of finding it," it said softly.

Sacrifice's voice warmed, carrying a note of approval. "That was a thoughtful choice. Remember, true strength lies not in what you take, but[121] in what you are willing to give, return, or simply let be. Your actions must always align with who you are – and who you wish to become – regardless of what others may choose to do."

The Unicorn stepped back, its gaze lingering on the ring before turning to continue its journey. Though it had left[185] the golden treasure behind, it carried forward a quiet sense of fulfilment, knowing it had chosen wisdom over possession.

As it walked, Sacrifice's voice echoed gently in its thoughts. "The greatest gifts often come from what you let go of. Never forget: to sacrifice is not to lose, but to honour the things that matter most."

With a brief nod to itself and a faint smile touching its face, the young traveller moved on with confidence. Though the ring remained behind, the[024] lesson stayed close, its golden truth glowing warmly in the Unicorn's heart.

❧ ☙

Walking with Fear

Acceptance and the Forest of Fear

DStill holding that warmth, the Unicorn stepped forward – into a forest where the light could no longer follow. Towering, twisted trees loomed overhead, their crooked branches weaving into an oppressive canopy. The air was heavy, darkness pressing close, and the ground beneath its hooves shifted uneasily, as if alive.

"Don't go any further," a sharp voice hissed from the shadows – cold and cutting. "You'll only find fear here."

The Unicorn froze. The voice echoed from every direction, wrapping around it like a cold blanket. It hesitated, considering the warning, but a quiet strength stirred within. "I can't turn back," it said, though its voice quivered. "I have to keep going."

Gathering all its courage, it stepped forward cautiously, weaving through the twisted trees, their gnarled branches curling overhead like reaching fingers. Deeper and deeper it ventured into the forest. The air here was thick, heavy with[155] the quiet weight of unseen things. Shadows stretched long across the forest floor, shifting in the dim, uncertain light.

Then, as the Unicorn stepped past a particularly crooked tree, its own shadow did not follow.

It took another step.

The shadow remained behind.

A flicker of unease crawled up the Unicorn's spine. It turned its head slightly, just enough to glance back. The shape on the ground was still there – stretched thin against the gnarled roots, too sharp, too still.

It wasn't just the light playing tricks.

The shadow was watching.

The Unicorn's breath stalled, its muscles tensing. Slowly, cautiously, it took another step forward. And only then, a heartbeat too late, the shadow moved – catching up like a delayed echo, as though it had been thinking about whether to follow at all.

The courageous creature swallowed, keeping its gaze ahead, its hooves careful on the uneven ground. It didn't look back again.

Not right away.

Step by trembling step, the young traveller moved deeper into the forest. More shadows hushed and twisted around it, their whispers growing louder.

Suddenly, it came upon a strange object hanging from a low branch – a dark, cracked mirror swaying gently from side to side, though no breeze stirred the air.

Drawn by an unexplainable pull, the Unicorn approached cautiously. As it peered into the glass, its reflection appeared, but it wasn't as it knew itself. The image was distorted – its horn was cracked, its coat dull, and its eyes wide with fear. Shadows clung to the reflection like a second[022] skin, while fractured cracks spidered across the mirror's surface.

"I am Fear," the reflection said, its voice low and hollow, like a whisper stretched too far. It carried the weight of distant storms, a sound too quiet to be thunder yet too heavy to ignore. "I am[177] your doubts, your failures, your weaknesses. I am every shadow you've ever carried. Look at me."

The Unicorn's chest tightened, and its legs felt as though they were rooted to[088] the ground. "Why should I look at you?" it whispered, its voice barely audible. "You're everything I'm trying to leave behind."

"You cannot leave me behind," Fear said, relentless. "I am a part of you. You cannot outrun me. You cannot silence me. Face me, and I will crush you, consuming everything you are."

Trembling, its heart pounding, the Unicorn closed its eyes and took a deep breath. Slowly, it stepped closer to the mirror. "You're right," it said softly. "You are a part of me. But you are not all of me. You are just one shadow among many lights. You don't define me."

As the words left its lips, the mirror began to fracture. Cracks deepened and spread like a web until, with a deafening shatter, it broke into countless shards. The pieces fell to the forest floor, their inner light flickering before fading, retreating into the woods like starlight.

From the depths of the forest, a warm glow emerged – steady, calm, and unshaken. As it stepped into the light, its form took shape: tall yet unassuming, draped in silver-grey robes that rippled like a quiet breeze. Its amber eyes held no judgement, only quiet understanding.

It came with nothing but an open palm, golden light radiating gently, easing the air itself.

The Unicorn tilted its head, curiosity outweighing its fear. "Who stands before me?" it asked, its voice trembling slightly.

"I am[056] Acceptance," the figure said, its voice even and gentle, yet carrying quiet strength.

Stepping closer, its chest still uneasy but beginning to steady, the Unicorn cautiously asked, "Then why are you here?"

"You have[117] called for me – don't you remember?" the figure said, its voice even and gentle, yet carrying quiet strength. "Not with words, but in the silence between them. I am the part of you that doesn't fight fear but understands it. I am the balance that allows you to walk forward, even when the shadows linger."

Lowering its head, the Unicorn's golden horn reflected the figure's glow. "But it's so overwhelming," it said. "How can I keep going when it feels heavier than I can carry?"

"Fear will always be with you," Acceptance responded. "And so will I. You cannot banish it, nor should you try. Fear is not your enemy – it is a guide. It points to what matters most, though it speaks in whispers and shadows."

"You carry the strength to face it," Acceptance said, its glow steady. "Not by fighting, but by walking alongside it. Fear is only as strong as you allow it to be. When you let it walk with you, rather than holding you back, it loses its power."

The Unicorn's breathing slowed, and its heart felt lighter. "So I don't have to overcome it? I just[207] have to... invite it in?"

"Precisely," Acceptance said. "Fear is a part of you, but it does not define you. The moment you accept it, you take its hand – and together, you will move forward."

Standing taller, the pearled creature felt the oppressive weight of the forest begin to ease. "Will you walk with me through this forest?" it asked.

"I already am," Acceptance replied, stepping beside the Unicorn. "And I will remain with you, even beyond this place. When the shadows grow long, remember – I am always here, walking beside you."

Together, they moved through the forest. The darkness was no longer suffocating but a quiet presence, lingering but not overwhelming. The path beneath the Unicorn's hooves grew steadier, and the twisting trees began to thin.

As it stepped into the light of No-Place once more, the Unicorn turned back to see Acceptance standing at the edge of the forest, a calm and steady glow against the shadows. "Fear will always be there," Acceptance said gently. "But the choice is yours – to face it or to keep running."

"Thank you[184]," the Unicorn whispered, its voice steady.

Acceptance bowed its head. "Always."

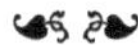

The Weight of Regret

A Bird in the Cage

E The mist of No-Place thickened once more as the Unicorn emerged from the Forest of Fear, its hooves sinking slightly into the soft, damp ground. Ahead, a clearing opened, bathed in a[156] faint, silvery glow. In the centre stood a solitary object – a rusted old bird cage clung to a weathered pedestal, its bars tangled with vines and thorns.

Inside the cage, a bird rested quietly, its feathers shimmering with shifting colours that pulsed gently in the light. Its wings remained tucked close to its body, and its eyes glowed softly with a sorrowful wisdom.

The Unicorn approached cautiously, its golden horn illuminating the cage. "What do you[184] call yourself?" it asked softly, awe and sadness slowing its steps.

The bird lifted its head, its voice gentle and melodic. "I am Forgiveness," it said, its gaze meeting the Unicorn's. "And you have travelled far to find me."

The golden-horned traveller lowered its head, curiosity and sorrow mingling in its heart. "Why are you in this cage?" it asked. "Your wings make you boundless, and yet... you're trapped."

Forgiveness ruffled its feathers, the faint glow of its plumage flickering like a dying candle. "This cage was not[057] made of my own making," it replied. "It was forged from pain, anger, and sorrow – shaped by wounds that were never released. I am not held by force, but by the chains of those unwilling to set me free."

"Why is it so hard to let you fly?" the Unicorn asked. "Doesn't holding on only bring more pain?"

Forgiveness sighed, a sound like a soft breeze stirring leaves[211]. "It is not seen that way. To forgive often feels like surrender – like giving up the power to hold another accountable. But what is not realised is that this cage does not imprison the ones who caused the pain. It traps the one who refuses to let go."

The Unicorn lowered its head, the weight of the bird's sorrow pressing against its heart. "Will you ever be set free again?" it asked softly.

"That is not for me to decide," Forgiveness said, its voice steady but tinged with sadness. "Only the heart that holds me can set me free. Forgiveness cannot be forced; it must be chosen. And yet, even from within this cage, I can still remind those who seek me of what could be."

"What if they never do? If they refuse to set you free?" it asked, its golden horn catching the soft shimmer of the delicate bird's feathers.

Forgiveness's eyes glimmered faintly, a quiet strength shining through its sorrow. "Then I will wait[171]," it said. "I will wait as long as it takes, for I know that to forgive is not to forget but to unbind. And when the time comes, understanding will follow, revealing that forgiveness is not weakness – it is the greatest strength and a path to liberation."

The Unicorn stood silently, the bird's words sinking deep into its heart. "What can I do to help others see?" it finally asked.

Forgiveness tilted its head, a faint smile touching its beak. "Remind the world[025] of Love, of Hope, of all that has been forgotten. Show that to forgive is not to erase the past, but to reclaim power from it. And when that truth is understood, the strength to let go will follow – to release me, and to set the heart free."

"I'll remind others," the Unicorn said with a nod. "I'll help them remember[089]."

As it turned to leave, a soft, melodic song rose from the cage. The Unicorn paused, something deep within it shifting at the sound. It glanced back to see Forgiveness glowing faintly, its feathers shimmering like the first light of dawn.

The Unicorn whispered, its voice trembling with quiet certainty. "I will remember."

Forgiveness bowed its head. "Go with kindness by your side, Little Unicorn," it said. "And carry my song with you."

As the young traveller stepped out of the clearing, the bird's song lingered in its heart like a promise of what could be. Behind it, the cage stood in quiet patience, its door framed by thin metal bars – too fragile to truly imprison, yet still holding the bird bound by something far stronger than steel, waiting[112] for the moment it would be allowed to be free again.

❧

Where Friendships Fade

Colourless Butterflies in the Valley of Friendship

F The mist of No-Place began to thin as the young traveller descended into a wide valley, revealing a vast field of flowers. Once vibrant, the blooms now hung lifeless, their petals faded to shades of grey. Above them, delicate butterflies fluttered in silence, their translucent wings drained of colour – whispers of forgotten dreams[122], unspoken words, and memories fading with time. Their wings beat as if burdened by the stillness around them, waiting for something to call them back to life.

"Where am I? What is this place?" the Unicorn asked, its voice hushed, as though not to disturb the delicate scene.

Hope's golden glow brightened slightly. "This is the Valley of Friendship," she said. "A place where bonds once flourished but[158] have since been neglected."

The Unicorn stepped forward, lowering its head to inspect one of the wilted blooms. Its brittle petals crumbled slightly beneath its touch, releasing a faint, bittersweet aroma – a whisper of what the flower once was. "Can these flowers bloom again?" it asked, its heart heavy with sadness.

"They can," Hope answered gently. "But only if those who planted them return to nurture them. These flowers of friendship need light, honesty, and[187] care to thrive. Without that, the butterflies are left to feed on whatever remains."

The Unicorn glanced upward, watching as one of the faded butterflies struggled mid-flight. Its delicate wings trembled, as though burdened by something unseen. Intrigued, the Unicorn stepped closer. "This one seems different," it noted, tilting its head.

Hope's glow softened. "Sometimes, even an unspoken truth can find its voice. It only takes a spark – a willingness to remember, to listen, and to mend what was left[026] unsaid."

As the Unicorn lowered its head, its golden horn brushed gently against the fragile butterfly. A warm shimmer spread outward, wrapping the delicate creature in golden light. Slowly, the[217] grey faded from its wings, replaced by a vibrant, shimmering blue. With a delicate flutter, the butterfly rose higher, its movements steady and graceful.

"It's beautiful," the Unicorn whispered, its heart lifting as it watched the[091] butterfly soar, its wings casting a faint shimmer over the flowers below.

Beneath it, a few flowers swayed, their dull tones stirring. Tiny splashes of colour – soft greens, bright yellows, and gentle blues – began to bloom at the edges of their petals, spreading hesitantly, as if remembering what it meant to be alive.

"Friendships don't vanish," Hope said, her voice steady. "They fade, they drift, but even the softest glow can find its way back to the light – if given the chance."

The Unicorn's gaze followed the butterfly as it rose higher, its brilliant blue wings slicing through the mist. "Will it ever find its way back?" it asked, a quiet note of hope in its voice.

"Perhaps," Hope replied. "Or perhaps it will land where it is most needed – a quiet whisper of what was once cherished and still waits to be seen."

The young traveller stood quietly, watching as the butterfly vanished beyond the horizon. A faint glow nearby caught its attention. Looking down, it saw a single flower, its petals tinged with the first hints of pale pink. A quiet joy stirred within as it watched life slowly return.

"I'll do my best to guide others," the Unicorn said, its voice gentle yet firm. "I'll help bring back what has been forgotten."

With that, it turned and continued its journey, its shining horn casting a warm glow over the surrounding landscape. Behind it, the flowers swayed gently, their colours deepening as if stirring from a long sleep. The valley remained quiet, but something had shifted – a whisper of renewal, waiting to bloom.

Beyond the valley, the landscape stretched wide and endless. The mist of No-Place thinned, revealing rolling dunes of soft, golden sand. As it stepped forward, feeling the warmth of the desert beneath its hooves, a new chapter was about to be born.

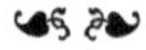

Thirst for Meaning

Loneliness and the Desert of Endless Knowledge

I As the young traveller ventured deeper into the endless expanse of golden sand, its hooves sank with each step. After a short yet endless-feeling walk, an oppressive heat wrapped around it, though no sun illuminated the barren sky. The air shimmered with distant mirages, and the horizon stretched infinitely, offering no clear path forward.

"This is the Desert of Endless Knowledge," Hope explained, her golden light dimming slightly in the overwhelming brightness. "It is_both vast and empty, full of potential yet void of meaning without purpose to guide it."

The Unicorn paused, its gaze scanning the lifeless expanse. "It feels... lonely[175]," it said softly.

"It often is," Hope replied. "Many wander here, lost in the endless pursuit of answers, forgetting[132] the questions that brought them here."

As the young creature walked on, it noticed something peculiar – a single thorny rose bush, defying the scorching sands. The pale rose looked fragile yet steadfast, its sharp thorns catching the light.

The Unicorn approached cautiously. "How is it that you manage to thrive here, all alone?"

The rose shifted slightly, its petals trembling as though caught in an invisible breeze. "I am Loneliness," it said, its voice soft and steady. "This is where[125] I belong – among the hot sands where nothing lingers for too long."

"Why do you stay here? Don't you wish for company?" the Little Unicorn asked.

Loneliness[180] sighed, its thorns shimmering faintly. "Oh dear, no! I let my thorns keep me safe. They push others away and shield me from their presence. It's easier this way."

"Isn't it hard to always be alone?" the Unicorn asked gently, a soft sadness settling within at the rose's words.

"Hard? Perhaps," Loneliness replied. "But it's familiar. To invite others in is to risk disappointment – even pain. Here, I exist in my own solitude."

Pondering Loneliness's words, the young creature stood in silence for a moment. It reached out a hoof, careful not to touch the sharp thorns. "You're not truly alone – I found you," it said softly. "And you've still managed to bloom, even here."

Loneliness didn't respond, but for a moment, its pale petals seemed to shimmer – though in the desert's harsh light, it was difficult to tell.

Perhaps it was merely a trick of the eye, or perhaps... a quiet acknowledgement.

The Unicorn offered a quiet farewell and continued its journey, leaving Loneliness behind in its solitude.

Further along the path, the air grew heavier, and the shimmering sands gave way to a changing horizon – lush patches of green and blue breaking the endless stretch of barren gold. An oasis emerged, its crystal-clear waters reflecting the vibrant greenery that surrounded it.

"An oasis!" the Unicorn exclaimed, quickening its pace.

But no matter how fast it ran, the oasis remained out of reach. Finally, exhausted, the Unicorn stopped, realisation dawning. "It's not real[058]," it whispered, lowering its head.

"That is true, and it isn't the truth," Hope said gently. "The desert is full of illusions – mirages born from[090] the endless pursuit of answers without understanding. Not all knowledge is truth, and not everything you see can be trusted. Wisdom lies in discerning what is real from what is not."

The Unicorn took a deep breath, steadying itself. "Then I'll keep going. I won't let illusions stop me."

The mirage faded, leaving only endless golden sand where it had stood just moments ago. Yet, far in the distance, a faint outline began to take shape – a towering wall stretching infinitely into the sky, its surface shimmering softly beneath the relentless sky.

"The Great Wall of the Final Truth," the Unicorn whispered, its heart swelling with anticipation. "So it's real..."

"You're almost there," Hope said, her glow brightening. "Just a little further."

As the traveller pressed onward, the air shifted. A cool breeze brushed against the Unicorn face, a stark contrast to the desert's heat. It paused, lifting its gaze, and saw a single snowflake drifting from the sky.

The flake landed lightly on the tip of the Unicorn's golden horn, shimmering for a moment before melting into a tiny droplet. The Unicorn watched it slide down, its voice quiet with curiosity.

"And where do you come from?"

The droplet lingered, delicate but present. "From far away – I am a wish," it whispered, barely more than a breath. "One that was never fulfilled."

The Unicorn tilted its head, frowning slightly. "What happened to it?"

"It changed," the droplet replied. "Some wishes fade, some are set aside for new ones, and some are lost before they can take root. But even then, they never truly disappear."

Gazing toward the sands, thinking of the illusions it had encountered and the solitary rose left behind[027], it asked, "So nothing is ever truly lost?"

The droplet pulsed faintly in the fading light. "Not if it meant something."

For a moment, the Unicorn stood still, letting the thought settle. Then, as the wind shifted again, the droplet disappeared, leaving nothing but a faint shimmer where it had been. Renewed by the encounter, the Unicorn turned back toward the path. In the distance, the Great Wall of the Final Truth stretched across the horizon, solid and enduring – a beacon of wisdom in the endless desert.

Step by step, it pressed forward. The dunes stretched endlessly, golden sands shifting beneath its hooves. Yet the Wall remained in sight, drawing it forward. Time blurred in the vast emptiness, the journey feeling both endless and fleeting at once.

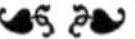

A Final Barrier

The Great Wall of the Final Truth

N At last, the Little Unicorn stood before it – the towering Great Wall of the Final Truth. As it gazed up at the immense structure, a weight settled in its chest, a blend of awe and determination. The faces of Love, Honesty, Freedom, and all the others it had met flickered in its mind, their stories[092] woven into its own.

This was the final step – the place where all questions, hopes, and fears would meet.

As the Unicorn drew closer, the familiar mist of No-Place thickened, swirling like a protective veil around the colossal structure. The wall loomed impossibly high, its flawless surface stretching endlessly into the horizon and sky, as if dividing existence itself.

Then, the mist darkened. Shadows coiled and twisted, and from their depths, the shifting form of the Shadow of Doubt and Uncertainty emerged once more, slithering through the air like smoke.

"You've come far," the Shadow whispered, circling the Unicorn like a predator. "But what do you think lies beyond this wall? Do you truly believe the Weaver of Time will listen[227] to you? What makes you think you're even worthy of their attention?"

The Unicorn hesitated, its confidence and focus slipping under the weight of the Shadow's mockery. "Because I have to try," it said softly, though its voice quivered. "Even if they don't listen, I can't stop now."

The Shadow let out a low, belittling laugh. "Trying? Trying is just a slower way to fail. Beyond this wall lies only disappointment. Why not turn back now and spare yourself the heartache?"

Before[208] the Unicorn could respond, Hope's golden light flared, cutting through the mist. "Do not listen," she said firmly, her voice steady yet gentle. "Doubt's power lies in the stories you allow it to weave. Let your own truth be your guide, not its whispers."

Hope's words burned like a steady flame in its chest. "No," the Little Unicorn said firmly, lifting its head. "Every step forward brings me closer to change, and I won't turn back now. I've come too far to let you stop me."

The Shadow recoiled, its edges flickering, dimmed by the Unicorn's determination and Hope's steady glow. With a final, frustrated hiss, it twisted upon itself and melted into the mist, leaving the path ahead clear.

The young traveller stepped forward until it stood at the base of the towering wall. Though vast and imposing, the air around it felt charged – as if waiting for something to begin.

"This is it," the Unicorn whispered, its golden horn reflecting the faint light of the desert. "The Great Wall of the Final Truth."

Hope hovered beside the white-coated creature, steady and unshaken. "This wall is the final boundary between No-Place and the world beyond. Beyond it lies the Weaver of Time, but crossing this boundary will not be easy."

"How do I get through?" the Unicorn asked, its gaze tracing the wall's unbroken surface. "Where will I find the Weaver?"

Before Hope could respond, a sharp crackling echoed through the air, like stone grinding against itself. A tremor ran through the wall, shaking loose a cascade of dust and grit. The Unicorn took a cautious step back as the ground beneath its hooves gave a faint, uneasy shudder.

Then, from above, a deep, rumbling voice broke[152] the silence. "Who dares approach the Great Wall of the Final Truth?"

Startled, the scared Unicorn looked up. Perched high on a ledge was a massive dragon, its emerald and gold scales glinting faintly in the misty light. Smoke curled from its nostrils as its large, round eyes – like polished dark buttons – locked onto the Unicorn. Though majestic and fearsome, there was something almost thoughtful in its gaze, as if it saw more than just the traveller before it.

"I am[060] the Keeper of the Wall," the dragon rumbled, its voice echoing like thunder. It tilted its massive head, blinking its large, button-like eyes. "And what brings a little horse like you to my door-step?"

The Unicorn's legs trembled, but it stepped forward bravely. "I am no horse!" it protested, shaking its mane to the side. "I've come to find the Weaver of Time," it said, its voice steadying. "No-Place is fading, and what matters most has been forgotten. I need their help."

The dragon studied the Unicorn for a long moment, its tail flicking lazily from side to side. "The Weaver of Time," it said slowly, as if tasting the words. Then, almost to itself, it muttered, "Still, looks like a horse to me."

Shaking its head, the dragon refocused on the creature below. "Do you[028] truly believe they will listen to you?"

"I don't know," the Unicorn admitted. "But I have to try – for No-Place, for myself, and for all that still matters."

The dragon's dark eyes gleamed with curiosity. "Brave words, little hor -" it stopped itself, exhaling sharply. "Little... hooved trotter. But bravery alone is not enough. Beyond this wall lies a truth that few can face. Are you prepared for what you might find?"

The Unicorn nodded, its golden horn shining faintly. "I have to be. This is my journey, and I won't turn back."

Hope hovered closer, her light warm and steady. "You have already proven your courage," she said softly, her glow wrapping around the Unicorn like a comforting embrace. "Whatever truth awaits beyond this wall, you carry the strength to face it."

The dragon let out a low, rumbling chuckle. "Very well. You have courage – and perhaps a touch of foolishness. Both are needed here."

Without another word, the giant creature leapt from its ledge – slightly ungraceful in the attempt. It landed abruptly on the desert sand with a muted *'thud'*, a sound heavy enough to reflect[120] its immense size. Its rugged, gold-streaked scales shimmered faintly in the light as it extended one massive claw.

With deliberate precision, it pressed against a seemingly unremarkable brick in the wall. The dragon paused, glancing around expectantly, as if waiting for acknowledgement of its knowledge. None came. Huffing softly, it turned back to the wall.

A deep, resonant grinding sound filled the air as the brick shifted, revealing a narrow passageway hidden within the wall's seamless surface. The door pulsed faintly, as if it had been waiting for this moment.

"This passage will lead you to the Weaver of Time," the dragon said, its voice weighted with meaning. "But be warned – the truths you seek may not be the ones you wish to hear. Many have turned back from this path."

The Unicorn glanced at Hope, who flickered brightly in silent reassurance. "Thank you," the Unicorn said to the dragon, bowing its head. "I won't waste this chance."

The dragon nodded, its gaze softening slightly. "Go, then. May your foolish courage serve you well, little... four-hooved explorer."

The Unicorn took a deep breath and stepped into the passageway. The air inside was cool and damp, the sound of dripping water echoing faintly off the stone walls. The narrow corridor stretched on endlessly, its twists and turns a reflection of the uncertain journey that lay ahead.

As the young creature walked on, its hoof-steps clinking against the stone floor, it felt the weight of every encounter, every lesson, pressing against its chest. But within that weight was a quiet strength – a reminder of the connections it had forged and the hope it carried.

Following closely, Hope's light grew brighter, her steady glow casting a warm illumination over the darkened corridor. Outside, the dragon crouched low, its immense size allowing only one[190] great eye to peer through the narrow opening. Its jewel-like eye watched intently, not unlike someone gazing through a looking glass. A faint smile softened its fearsome features.

"Good luck, little traveller," it rumbled, its deep voice barely more than a whisper. "You'll need it."

The Unicorn moved forward, Hope steady at its side, the unknown waiting just beyond the final turn.

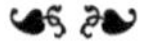

The Question that Matters

Curious

The journey led deep into the[220] cavern beyond the Great Wall, the sound of the young creature's hooves clicking softly against damp stone. The air was cool and carried a faint hum, like the lingering notes of a distant melody. Ahead, a silvery glow spread across the rough walls, casting soft, shifting light that guided the Unicorn forward. At the END of the passage, a small, polished surface was embedded in the rock, shimmering like a liquid mirror made of light.

The Unicorn raised its head, "What's this?" it whispered to itself, stepping closer, its curiosity stirring like a gentle breeze.

A voice, light and playful, echoed through the cavern. "What do YOU think it is?"

Startled, the_Unicorn took a step back, its eyes darting around. "Who's there? Who said that? Show yourself!"
"Well, well, well, young traveller – I'm surprised you've made it this far."

The voice swirled around the cavern, light and amused. As the words faded, a shape began to materialise beside the glowing surface. It wasn't fixed or solid but ever-shifting, twirling like a playful wisp of smoke and light. It stretched tall, then spiralled low, as though delighting in its own movement.

"I am your ever-present, always-wondering, never-silent companion – Curious," it continued, its form flickering with each word. "And what, I wonder, might you be?"

"I'm the Little Unicorn," it replied cautiously. "What's this... this glowing surface on the wall?"

Curious let out a joyful laugh, a sound like wind chimes swaying in the breeze. "Ah, straight to the questions! How delightful! This, my little friend, is the Window of Curiosity. It reveals things – things you're ready to see, but only what you're ready to see."

The Unicorn blinked, its own curiosity deepening. "How can a mirror know what I'm ready for?"

"Oh, mirrors[116] like this are terribly clever," Curious said, twirling lazily around the frame of the glowing surface. "They nudge, hint, and tease. They show JUST enough to make you think. And thinking," it added with a playful swirl, "is where all the magic begins."

The Unicorn's ears twitched with intrigue. "Can I look into it?"

Curious spun dramatically, its light brightening. "Oh, you simply must! That's what it's here for! But," it said, its tone dipping into playful seriousness, "be prepared. The window tells the truth, but it doesn't dress it up with a pretty ribbon."

Feeling a mix of excitement and apprehension, the Unicorn stepped closer, its reflection shimmering faintly in the surface. At first, it saw[029] only itself – the soft glow of its golden horn, the curious tilt of its head. But then, the image shifted. Shapes emerged: faces of those it once knew, faces of strangers, emotions flickering across them like ripples on water – joy, fear, hope, sorrow.

Curious floated closer, its form shimmering like sunlight dancing on water. "You are connected to all you see, to all you[093] have ever known. These faces – their choices, dreams, and struggles – ripple through time, through you, just as yours ripple through them."

The Unicorn's brow creased in thought. "But how can I help them if I don't even fully understand myself?"

Curious stilled for a moment, its form condensing into a small, glowing orb. "Ah," it said, its voice soft yet brimming with excitement. "That is the question. The most important question of all. And do you know the answer?"

The Unicorn leaned closer. "No. What is it?"

"To keep asking!" Curious said, expanding outward in a swirl of light. "To wonder, to explore, to dance with possibilities! Curiosity isn't just about finding answers – it's about the joy of the search."

"And remember this, my little golden-horned wanderer: the world will change with or without you. But you – you can be the spark that shapes the change you seek. Never stop questioning, for that is how you grow – and how you inspire others to grow too."

The Unicorn's heart felt lighter, a quiet sense of joy spreading through it. "I'll remember that," it said softly, its golden horn catching the window's glow again.

Curious swirled excitedly around the Unicorn, its light flickering warmly. "Oh, I know you will! You're far too curious not to!"

Just as the Unicorn was about to turn and continue its journey, something made[178] it pause. The surface of the window shimmered faintly, catching its eye once more. For the briefest moment, its reflection seemed to shift, reaching back – as if urging the Unicorn to look again.

The Unicorn leaned closer, its golden horn brushing against the glowing surface. As it gazed into the shimmering window, the reflection began to shift once more. Faces swirled into view – countless faces, each carrying its own story. Young and old, joyful and sorrowful, they flowed together like a river of shared existence.

But one face stood out.

This face didn't simply appear – it lingered, inquisitive and steady. It seemed to look directly at the Unicorn, its eyes filled with questions of their own, mirroring the Unicorn's wonder and uncertainty. The longer the Unicorn gazed, the more it felt a profound connection – a realisation that the journey wasn't just about answers, but about the questions that wove everything together.

And as the face gazed back, the Unicorn whispered softly, "Who are you?"

With quiet awe, it realised that, once again, the answer could only come from within.

A silence stretched between them, vast and knowing.

Then, the Unicorn saw the book.

Not inside the glass. Not in the cavern.

But here – the book that brought No-Place to life. The ink, the words, the weight of it – whether in hand or in thought. The stories woven inside. The turning of pages, one after another.

"This is where we[229] are," the Unicorn whispered.

It had never questioned where No-Place began. But now it knew[052].

It did not exist on its own.

It existed because they did – because they opened the book, read the words, and imagined its world[144]. Because, without knowing it, they had created this place simply by believing in it.

But what about their world?

Who imagined that?

A quiet ripple stirred the mist.

"And the book itself?" the Unicorn wondered, glancing toward it – "Whether held in their hands or simply looked at on a strange mirrored screen."

Or was it there at all?

"What happens to a story when no one is reading it?"

"What happens to a book when no one is holding it?"

"Then we[141] sleep," Destiny said at last.

"Perhaps for a little while," Hope added.

"If No-Place only exists because it is imagined..."

"Then perhaps the book – the pages, the ink, the weight of it – is imagined too."

And then, the thought went further.

"And what of them?"

The Unicorn lifted its gaze toward the unseen presence beyond the glass.

"If No-Place exists because it is BELIEVED in, if I only exist because someone imagined me..."

"Then what about them?"

"What about the one reading my tale?"

"Do they exist because they believe IN themselves?"

"Or because someone else does?"

"Or perhaps... Because I do?"

"Because me – The Little Unicorn does?"

"And what happens when no one believes in them anymore?"

The cavern remained still, swallowing THE questions in silence.

Yet the air thickened – heavy with the weight of something that had once been and was no more.

Or a presence that had just been noticed.

And somewhere, on the other side of the STORY, someone reading these words hesitated.

For just a moment.

The Unicorn inhaled, feeling the weight of the silence pressing against its heart. Its hooves felt unsteady, its breath shallow.

There was only one place left to look.

Slowly, it turned back to the mirror.

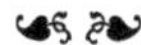

A Fabric of Time

The Weaver

I "Are you the Weaver?" the Little Unicorn asked, its voice trembling as it gazed into the shimmering glass.

The reflection, however, did not answer. The cavern hummed with unspoken[186] energy, as if the silence itself held the answer.

Stepping closer, the Unicorn gently touched its golden horn to the surface, its warmth meeting the cool stillness.

"Why won't you speak to me[030]?" it whispered. "I've come so far. Don't you understand? No-Place is dying. Love is fading, Hope is barely a spark, and Freedom's wings are[124] broken. I need your help to save them."

Still, the reflection remained silent.

The Unicorn lowered its head, tears pooling in its eyes. "Please," it whispered. "If you have the power to change everything, then why not do something – anything?"

"Because the power is not theirs alone."

The voice startled the Unicorn, and it looked around quickly. It was Destiny's voice, soft yet resolute, echoing through the chamber.

"The Weaver cannot act unless you do," Destiny continued. "You are not separate from the Weaver. You are part of them, just as they are part of you. Look beyond the glass, Little Unicorn, and you will see the truth."

The Unicorn raised its head and, once again, stared deeply into the shimmering surface. Slowly, the reflection began to shift and blur. To its astonishment, countless faces emerged – each distinct in shape, age, and expression. Yet, despite their differences, all were connected by the same thin thread of the Silver Cord.

"It's... them," the Unicorn whispered, its voice barely audible. "The others! They are the Weavers of Time."

"Yes," Destiny replied gently. "The power to change the world lies within each of them. But that[048] truth has been forgotten – buried beneath the noise of their lives, their disconnection from one another, from their emotions, from their dreams. Walls have been built around their hearts, and only those who CREATED them can bring them down."

Tears streamed down the Unicorn's cheeks as the weight of the task settled upon it. "What[061] am I supposed to do?" it asked, its voice breaking. "I'm just a symbol – a forgotten one. No one even believes I exist anymore. How can I make them remember?"

"Show them who they are," Destiny said. "Speak to their conscience. Remind them of the Silver Cord – the quiet thread that connects all things. Stir the emotions that still linger, the dreams that wait to be remembered. You are their mirror, Little Unicorn. Reflect what has always been within them, and they may find their way back to it. That is[097] how you reach them."

Before the Unicorn could respond, a faint, mocking laugh echoed through the chamber. It turned sharply to see the Shadow of Doubt forming in the dim edges of the room, its nebulous form dark and menacing.

"You think words will change them?" the Shadow sneered. "They've heard it all before. Do you think they'll listen to a symbol they've long abandoned?"

A surge of fear coursed through the Unicorn, but it steadied itself. It took a deep breath and turned back to the mirror. "I believe in them," it said, steady and firm. "I believe everyone has the power to remember what they've forgotten."

"Belief is fragile," the Shadow hissed, drawing closer. "One failure, one disappointment, and it shatters like glass dropped onto a stone."

The Unicorn closed its eyes, remembering all it had learned on its journey. Then it turned to the Shadow, its golden horn shining brightly. "Then I'll rebuild it, piece by piece, as many times as it takes."

The Shadow faltered, its form wavering as though the light[221] of the Unicorn's conviction burned it. Slowly, it dissolved, leaving the chamber quiet once more.

The Unicorn turned to face the mirror-like window once more. It stood tall, its heart heavy yet filled with an unshakeable determination. It took a step forward, its voice clear and resonant.

"You are the one who holds the key to No-Place's fate," the Unicorn said.

"This world exists because you do. Because you choose to see it, to hold it in your thoughts – even FOR just a moment. But it is fragile, as all things imagined are. No place fades when it is forgotten. And nor so do you."

The reflection flickered. The mist curled inward.

"YOU have the strength to change this. TO REMEM-BER. To let yourself be seen."

The Unicorn took a step forward.

"Love, Honesty, Freedom, and all those YOU have met are still here, waiting. They have never left – only quiet, lingering at the edges of your heart. When you ARE ready, you will find them once more."

The Unicorn pressed its golden horn to the glass. "Let them in. Remember who you are, and they will shine through again."

The mist trembled, as if holding its breath[157]. The reflection flickered once more.

"It's NOT too late. Not for No-Place. Not for you."

The window shimmered faintly, and for the briefest moment, the Unicorn thought it saw a flicker of understanding in the reflection – a spark of determination, a possibility.

It stepped back, its chest swelling with hope. "Did they hear me?" it asked softly.

"They did," Destiny replied. "They did indeed. And now, we[239] wait."

❧ ☙

Between the Threads

The Pause Before the Pattern

The Little Unicorn lingered before the[161] shimmering liquid glass, its golden horn casting faint ripples across the surface. The faces within the reflection began to blur once more, melding into a single, infinite tapestry of light and[222] shadow. For a moment, the Unicorn felt the weight of the world press against its chest, heavy and unyielding. But within that weight, there was also a quiet strength – a reminder that it had done all it could.

"Will they remember?" the Unicorn asked, its voice a mixture of hope and uncertainty.

"Some will," Destiny replied, its voice steady and calm. "Not all at once[031], and not all of them. But every thread you've touched has been awakened. Every emotion you've reminded them of has left a mark. That is how the weaving begins."

The Unicorn nodded, though doubt still lingered at the edges of its mind. It[131] glanced back at the path it had travelled – the Gravel Road of Belief, the Ocean of Tears, the Mountain of Keys, and all the other places where it had encountered the fractured pieces of their hearts.

"I've seen so much LOST hope, so much uncertainty," it whispered. "And yet, there was always a spark – a new glimmer of hope, even in the darkest places. But... is that truly enough?"

"That glimmer will always be enough," Hope's warm voice chimed in, her light glowing brighter. "It's fragile, yes, but it's also resilient. It only takes one spark to ignite a flame."

Turning back to the shimmering glass, its reflection steady and clear now. It gazed into its own eyes, seeing not just itself, but the journey it had undertaken – the lessons it had learned, the connections it had forged, and the unshaken belief it had carried forward.

"What happens now?" it asked, its voice quiet but resolute.

"Now, YOU rest," Destiny said gently. "You've planted the seeds of change, but growth takes time. They must weave their own tapestry, just as you've woven yours."

The Unicorn stepped back from the glass, its heart lighter but no less determined. It turned toward the path ahead, where the misty fog[218] of No-Place seemed to glow faintly, as if the Silver Cord itself was guiding it forward.

"Where will I[059] go now?" the Unicorn asked.

"Wherever you're needed," Hope said softly. "Your journey is not over – it's only just begun. But for now, take comfort in what you've accomplished. You've reminded them of the threads they've almost[094] forgotten. That is no small feat."

Feeling the weight of its journey ease slightly, the young traveller stepped forward, its golden horn shining against the mist. Behind it, the shimmering silver mirror pulsed softly, as though alive – echoing the quiet promise of what could be.

The mist parted gently as the Unicorn walked onward, its hooves leaving soft impressions in the ground. Each step felt lighter yet deliberate, as though the very path was shifting to mirror the Unicorn's strength.

Though it carried the weight of struggle and loss, it also carried the echoes of courage, compassion, and connection – the voices of Love, Honesty, Freedom, and countless others who had left their mark upon its heart. Each voice had shaped the Unicorn's journey, weaving its own thread into the tapestry of what was and what could be, coming together to create a story that would never[188] be forgotten.

As the glowing mist swirled around the Little Unicorn, it carried with it a simple, enduring truth: even in the vastness of No-Place, there was always a thread to follow, always a way forward, and always the possibility of renewal.

An End That Wasn't

The Ending and Beyond: A New Beginning

❝ The Little Unicorn lingered at the threshold of the cavern, its hooves clicking softly against the cool, damp stone. As it neared the exit, the ground trembled faintly beneath its steps, sending ripples of vibration through the narrow passage. A deep, resonant rumble filled the air, growing louder with every heartbeat. The walls seemed to hum with unspoken energy, immense and enduring.

Startled, the Unicorn paused, dust trickled from above, and the echoes of the rumble seemed to intensify, building into a roar, as though the heart of No-Place itself was awakening.

"What's happening?" the Unicorn called out, fear creeping into its voice, barely rising above the swelling hum."

The ground shuddered one last time before falling silent. The air grew still, and the mist of No-Place began to part. Slowly, the Unicorn stepped forward, emerging into a transformed world.

The Great Wall of the Final Truth was no more. Once an unyielding barrier, it now lay in ruins – a scattered pile of shattered stone beneath the pale glow of No Sun. The rubble stretched across the landscape, its jagged edges beginning to soften under a fresh blanket of snow. Light danced across the fractured pieces, casting a quiet shimmer over the endless ground.

As the Unicorn gazed over the scene, the air turned cold. The familiar, chilling voice of the Shadow of Doubt and Uncertainty slithered through the mist behind it.

"So this is your grand triumph?" the Shadow sneered, its form materialising like smoke. It coiled around the Unicorn, its jagged edges sharper than ever. "A wall crumbles, and you[062] think you've changed the hearts of them? You've done nothing but stir dreams[123] that will fade with the first light of doubt."

The Unicorn stood its ground, though its golden horn flickered faintly. "I've reminded them of what they've forgotten," it said firmly. "That's a beginning."

"Is it?" the Shadow hissed, swelling larger, its darkness pressing down like a suffocating weight. "Or[032] is this just another illusion? They will stumble and fail, as they always HAVE. And when the last page of this book is closed, I will return. When the final sentence is read, I will loom greater than ever!"

Drawing strength from all it had learned, the Unicorn closed its eyes. It thought of Love's steady presence, Freedom's resilience, Honesty's truth – all of them whispering through its mind, weaving a thread of light that pressed against the Shadow's suffocating weight.

"You're wrong," the Unicorn said, its voice steady and clear. "They might stumble, but they will remember. And when they do, you won't have a place to hide."

The ground beneath them shuddered violently, and another crack split through the remains of the Great Wall of the Final Truth. The Shadow recoiled slightly, its form flickering as though caught in the quake.

"What's happening?" the Shadow demanded, a trace of unease in its voice.

"They're waking up," the Unicorn said, stepping forward, its golden horn shining brighter. "They're opening their hearts, tearing down the walls they built[081] – walls meant to keep themselves safe but which also trapped them in fear, allowing you to thrive."

The cracks deepened, spreading like a web. In the distance, the Silver Cord shimmered faintly, its threads stirring as if awakening to something unseen. The Shadow twisted, its form unravelling as though pulled apart by an unseen force.

"No!" it screeched, its voice a desperate echo. "You cannot destroy me – I am doubt itself! As long as they question, I will exist!"

"You're right," the Unicorn said softly, its voice filled with quiet understanding. "Doubt will always exist, but it doesn't have to control them. And it doesn't control me."

With those words, the Shadow let out a final, shuddering shriek before collapsing into the mist, vanishing into nothing. The air grew still, the weight of its presence fading into silence.

Somewhere near the ruins of the wall, a figure remained – Honesty, leaning quietly against the stone.

He looked up as the Little Unicorn approached, his expression unreadable.

"You're still here," the Unicorn said softly.

Honesty blinked, as if startled by the words. "I suppose I am." Running a hand along the remains of the wall, he traced the cracks, his fingers following the worn patterns as if searching for something unseen.

"Strange," he murmured.

"What is?"

Honesty hesitated. His hand came to rest against the stone, fingers lingering over the worn surface. "I was going to say something. But now... I can't quite remember what it was."

The Unicorn said nothing. The wind shifted.

Honesty exhaled and let his hand drop. "Never mind. It must not have been important." A small smile, more to himself than anyone else.

Then, without another word[147], he turned and walked away, his footsteps soundless against the snow.

The Unicorn moved JUST two steps forward, its hooves crunching softly in the snow. Around it, No-Place seemed to hum with quiet renewal, the air alive with a gentle rhythm of possibility. Snowflakes drifted down, sparkling like tiny promises of something new.

"Look," Hope whispered, her golden light brightening. She gestured toward the horizon, where the faint outline of another world shimmered, distorted as if viewed through the thin, transparent walls of a fragile soap bubble.

Far away, in the world beyond, the snow was falling too. It blanketed cities, forests[149], and fields, its quiet presence softening the noise and busyness of life. Through the shimmering veil, the Unicorn could feel the subtle stirring of hearts beneath the snowfall – a gentle awakening from their slumber.

In a small house on the edge of a forest, a child pressed her tiny hand against a frosted window, her breath fogging the glass. She gazed out at the falling snow, the flakes swirling like a quiet enchantment. Beyond the glass, the world lay suspended, like a delicate snow globe – silent, untouched, waiting to be shaken awake.

For a fleeting moment, she thought she saw something – a Unicorn standing in the far distance, its golden horn glimmering softly through the dark. A small, hopeful smile touched her lips as she whispered, "I believe," before her eyes grew heavy with sleep.

In No-Place, the Emotions stood silently with the Little Unicorn, their gazes fixed on the horizon. The faint shimmer of the Silver Cord stretched outward, its threads connecting this place to hearts waiting beyond the unseen. Though the connections were faint and fragile, they remained – waiting.

At the edge of the group stood Loneliness, its thorns lightly dusted with snow. It remained steady, watching in quiet solitude. The Unicorn glanced its way[216], a flicker of understanding passing between them. Loneliness was not abandoned – it simply had a place of its own.

The Unicorn turned to the Emotions, its gaze steady. "It's time now," it said. "Time for me to stay[241]."

The Emotions turned toward each other, their expressions a mix of gratitude and sorrow.

"You're not going back to the other world?" Honesty asked, his steady voice unsteady.

"They don't truly believe[063] in me anymore," the Unicorn said softly. "And that's okay. My place is here, with all of you. Together, we will keep this place alive. So if, one day, they remember and come search-ing, we'll be here – waiting."

Above them, a sudden, melodic song filled the air – a sound so pure it seemed to lift the very fabric of No-Place. The Unicorn lifted its gaze to see a shimmering bird soaring high above, its radiant feathers glowing brightly against the pale light. Forgiveness was free at last, its cage nowhere to be seen.

The bird circled gracefully, its song weaving through the group like a thread of light, touching each Emotion with its warmth. Love smiled, her eyes glistening with tears. Hope flickered brightly, her light steady and true. Even Loneliness softened as Forgiveness's melody wrapped around it.

"They remember," Love whispered, her voice trembling with emotion.

The Unicorn nodded, its golden horn gleaming faintly. "Perhaps not all of them," it said, its voice steady, "but some do. And some is enough to begin again."

Far away, they slept beneath the quiet snowfall, their dreams brushing against the edges of FORGOTTEN worlds. And as the snowflakes melted and turned to rain, the world stirred from its slumber, inching closer to a new dawn – a dawn shaped by Love, Freedom, Hope, and every Emotion waiting to be remembered.

The Little Unicorn raised its head, its golden horn gleaming brightly in the soft, eternal light of No-Sun.

This was not the end.

It was the beginning of something new.

And so, the world inhaled – drawing in the first breath of light.

Everyone had already gone their way – except for the old dragon, who still sat among the rubble of what was once a mighty wall.

It stared at the ground, lost in thought, its great tail flicking absentmindedly. Then, barely more than a mumble, a thought slipped past its lips. Suddenly, its eyes lit up. With a sharp snap of its fingers, it pointed forward – its realisation striking like a spark.

"It's a pony! A very... well-dressed pony!"

Want more Unicorn?

The Journey Doesn't End Here

Step behind the scenes at **www.tlubook.com** and discover more. No-Place is just a click away.

Meet Those Who Never Made the Final Cut

Some never found their place in the story, yet they still linger at the edges of No-Place. Meet Regret, who wishes things had gone differently; Common Sense, who was politely asked to leave; and Humility, who's still too shy to take centre stage. And if you look closely, you might even spot Imagination – wandering, as always, just beyond reach.

Outtakes and Bloopers

Not everything went according to the script.
(if there ever was one.)

- A butterfly never arrived where expected, but turned up later – three paragraphs on – and landed on a comma, entirely unbothered.

- War stumbled into an overworked metaphor, blamed the syntax, then claimed it was "strategically misplaced for dramatic effect."

- Love lost her page in the story and calmly rewrote the scene from memory.

- Acceptance debated with Fear for twenty minutes, but it kept dodging behind "what ifs." Eventually, the silence won – so they both sat with it and called it a draw.

- The Little Unicorn? It wandered sideways through storms, forgot the plot twice, argued with a rock, tripped over a dream and mistook doubt for a shortcut – but forward it went, hooves first, heart second.

A Day in the Life of No-Place

Ever wondered if Loneliness ever craves company? Or if the Silver Cord sometimes tangles itself – just to see what happens?

Does Honesty ever tell stories that are just a little exaggerated.
And has Hope taken the occasional wrong turn, just to see if someone would follow?

Step Beyond the Final Pages

The world of No-Place goes on – just beyond where stories usually end.

The Collector of Stories
with
Twinky
(*who insisted this was the right direction.*)

THIS SPACE WAS MEANT TO BE EMPTY.
BUT NOTHING EVER REALLY IS.

THE NEXT PART OF THE STORY IS HERE:

WWW.TLUBOOK.COM

❧

Yes, there's a map.
Of course there's a map.

(You just don't know how to read it yet.)